CROSSCURRENTS

and Other Stories

Gerry Wilson
Gerry Wilson

Press 53
Winston-Salem

Press 53, LLC
PO Box 30314
Winston-Salem, NC 27130

First Edition

Cover design by Kevin Morgan Watson

Cover art, "untitled," Copyright © 2015
by Clay Jones, used by permission of the artist.

Author photo by Christina Cannon Boteler

This is a work of fiction. Names, characters, places, and incidents
are products of the author's imagination or are used fictionally.
Any resemblance to actual events, locales, or persons,
living or dead, is entirely coincidental.

Printed on acid-free paper
ISBN 978-1-941209-29-5

CROSSCURRENTS AND OTHER STORIES

For Austin, with love

ACKNOWLEDGMENTS

The author wishes to thank the editors of the publications where the following stories appeared.

"Appendix," *Crescent Review,* 1997

"Book of Lies," *Prime Number Magazine,* Issue 37, 2013

"From This Distance," *The Arkansas Review,* 1998

"Mating" won the 2014 Prime Number Magazine Award for Short Story and appeared in *Prime Number Magazine,* Issue 61, and in *Prime Number Magazine, Editors' Selections: Volume 4,* 2014

"Pieces," *Prime Number Magazine,* Issue 19, and *Prime Number Magazine, Editors' Selections: Volume 2,* 2012

"Signs," *Blue Crow,* April 2011

"Sparrow, Sparrow," *Night Train,* July 2015

"Wives," *Halfway Down the Stairs,* September 2010, and later as "Something Borrowed" in *Good Housekeeping,* October 2011

CONTENTS

MATING

The first time Gail ran away from Cleary Mayfield, she drove south across the Florida Panhandle to the Gulf and rented a room in a cheap motel three blocks from the beach. She rarely left the room, and when she did, she tucked her hair under a hat and wore sunglasses. She walked to the gas station where she bought junk food and beer. Nights, she lay awake and peeked out the drapes every time she heard a car in the lot, expecting Cleary's old van to come to a rolling stop in front of her room and shine its bright lights through the plate-glass window.

When Cleary didn't come, Gail wondered why. Maybe she'd done too good a job of disappearing, or maybe he didn't care enough to look for her. She didn't love Cleary. She craved him. She drank herself to sleep in the dusky hours of morning and dreamed a black leopard lay at her feet, his eyes forlorn.

The day she left the beach, heavy clouds gathered over the Gulf, bringing torrents of rain that seemed to carry her inland towards Cleary. She had stayed away long enough for the bruises to fade to yellow.

When she got off the interstate, she was still half an hour from the animal refuge Cleary owned. Virgin pine forest and swamp surrounded Animal World for miles and miles. The wilderness bred its own population of bobcats, deer, alligators, coyotes, armadillos, snakes, maybe even bears. Until the interstate opened up a few years ago, the old highway had been a major route to the coast. Now, not many people stopped at Animal World.

Near the refuge she saw the first hand-painted sign— ANIMAL—and then the others, a quarter of a mile apart—WORLD, STOP, and a hundred yards from the entrance, NOW! The signs had been Cleary's idea, but she had painted them. A tall wood fence hid the refuge from the highway. Painting it flamingo pink had been her idea.

Gail pulled around back. Cleary's van was there. She sat for a minute to let her heart calm down before she rummaged in her purse and found the key to the private gate. She unstuck her bare thighs from the vinyl seat and got out of the car. The minute she stepped inside, her eyes watered at the ammonia smell of urine, the sour-sweet stink of feces. Gone two weeks, and she'd forgotten just how bad it was.

The cages nearest the back of the compound held the big cats. Cleary had called it his anticipation strategy; let the customers see the other animals first and build up to the best part. They weren't real cages, but pens built out of chain-link fence. Fencing covered the tops, and each pen had a single, padlocked entry. Only the big cats' pens had concrete floors. Cleary aspired to have real cages, he had told her. Real cages were part of his long-range plan.

In the first pen—or the last, if you were a customer walking through—the male black leopard, Garcia, stopped pacing and leveled his yellow eyes at Gail. Those eyes sent heat through her, like a lover's.

"Hey there," she said. "How've you been, Garcia?" But she saw how he was. His feed pan was empty and dry. Big dumps littered the cage. Cleary must not have cleaned Garcia's pen at all while she was gone. The cat growled and rubbed against the chain-link. The light caught the variations in his blue-black coat, the rosettes of the spot pattern barely visible. He was beautiful, and he was partly hers.

After their only tiger died six months ago, Cleary had searched the Internet for a replacement. He had found the black cat on a private zoo's website in south Florida.

"A panther?" Gail said when he showed it to her.

He shook his head. "No such thing as a black panther. There's mostly black leopards or jaguars. This one's a leopard. It's a shame we can't buy him."

Gail saw the price. "I could pay some." An impulse, the words out of her mouth before she thought about it. She'd made good money working as a waitress at the Beau Rivage on the Gulf coast. Casino customers, especially older men, were big tippers. After she lost that job, she'd worked in one bar or another and spent maybe half of what she'd saved up, just to get by. She'd held on to the rest and never told anybody about it, until now.

He clicked off the screen. "Naw. I can't let you do that."

But Gail couldn't stop thinking about the black leopard. Except for her car—a clunker she'd bought while she had the casino job—she had never owned anything.

One night, in bed, she said, "Nothing on the refuge is mine. Let me help you buy the cat. He'd be, like, my stake in the place."

Cleary had given in, or maybe, she thought later, her paying had been his strategy all along. Whatever, she had withdrawn the money she'd managed to save while she'd worked at the casino—fifteen hundred dollars—and they had driven all the way to Fort Myers to buy the cat she'd named Garcia.

"We'll mate him," Cleary had said. "We'll make a fortune."

Now, Gail regretted bringing Garcia here. "I'll be back," she said to the cat. "I'll bring you something to eat, I promise."

In the next pen, the bobcat, Jewel, lay curled in the back corner, her eyes glassy and sticky with pus. Flies buzzed around her head, and she didn't bother to flick them off. A piece of rotting horsemeat lay a couple of feet away.

"*Cleary?*" Gail yelled. She walked towards the trailer she and Cleary lived in, checking the other pens as she passed. The orangutan lobbed shit at her. "Same to you, buddy," she said.

Cleary came out of the trailer. He wore a dirty muscle shirt and cut-off jeans and a few days' stubble of beard. His eyes looked hollowed out, like he hadn't been sleeping. Gail hoped he had learned something. Maybe he would think twice before he hit her again.

He said, "Well. Look who's here."

"Yeah. I'm glad to see you, too. Don't tell me you haven't noticed Jewel. And Garcia looks like he's starving."

"What was I supposed to do with you gone? I can't do it all."

"Meaning you won't. We should call the vet."

"It's the heat, Gail. Jewel's okay."

"I don't think so." Gail started up the trailer steps. He grabbed her arm.

"We can't have anybody like that coming in here. Not till we get things shaped up."

She looked at his hand. "Let go. That hurts."

He stepped back, running his hands through his hair. "Jesus," he said. "Damn." He pulled her to him and kissed her. "I about went crazy with you gone."

She wanted to push him away, she really did. Driving back, she had promised herself she would go slow with Cleary, take the measure of things, see how steady he was. But she had never been with a man like him. He was not a big man, and he wasn't handsome: he was lean and sunburned, sinewy and strong, as though he had been forged, not born. She had never seen eyes like his, green-gold and luminous in his weathered face, and once she met his gaze, once she felt his breath on her neck and his hands on her breasts and moving down, she forgot everything else.

He let her go, the space between them abrupt, cruel. *This is what I missed,* she told herself. *This is what I almost lost.*

"Where's your bag?" he said.

"In the car. I'll go get it."

"No. I'll do it later."

She went with him into the trailer.

The next morning, Gail left Cleary asleep and went out. She needed to keep busy so she wouldn't think too much. All he'd had to do was put his hands on her. She hadn't even fed the cats last night. "Slut," she said aloud. "Trash."

She unlocked Jewel's gate and tossed in a chunk of meat, but Jewel barely lifted her head. Garcia devoured his portion and looked at her like, Where's the rest? Turned from her with a growl, ambled the length of the pen, back and forth, back and forth.

There was no more meat; she'd given them the last in the cooler.

No sign of Cleary yet. She would clean the cages herself. She dragged a hose with a high-pressure nozzle to

Jewel's pen and washed it out. When the water hit the concrete in Garcia's cage, he spooked, roared, charged the chain-link. Gail shut the nozzle off.

"Hey," she said. "You're okay. It's okay now."

She had seen Cleary go right in there with the cats and sweep the pens out. He had forbidden her to do it, but she could. It was her fault that he'd neglected Garcia. If she hadn't gone away, everything would be fine. Well, no, that wasn't true. The place had been a mess before she left. Now it was worse.

She went to the shed and got the big broom and the heavy canvas coat and gloves Cleary wore when he went in the pens. She didn't believe Garcia would hurt her. Even so, her pulse drummed in her ears. Any cat could be dangerous. An agitated, hungry cat even more so.

She waited a while for the cat to settle down. Once he did, she filled a bucket with water, put on the coat and gloves, and picked up the broom and bucket. She opened Garcia's gate and stepped inside, closing it behind her. Garcia whirled and growled, then backed away. She remembered Cleary's posture when he went in the pens, his slow, smooth movements. Cleary was not one to look away. He engaged the cat's eyes and held them, like a circus trainer. He talked to the cats, his voice low and even. He'd been mauled once, almost lost an arm, he'd told her, but that was long before she came. "I'm smarter now," he'd said. "I'm more careful."

"It's all right, Garcia. You're all right," Gail said. "That's a good boy." She poured water on the floor and started sweeping the filth to the back of the pen. The muck stank something awful. She pushed it out through the chain-link, keeping the cat in her line of sight as best she could. Garcia paced the far side of the cage, grumbling, pawing at the fence. "Just a little more," Gail said. She brushed sweat out of her eyes and felt it trickle down her sides.

She heard a noise and turned, expecting the cat to be on her, but Garcia faced the path. Cleary was walking towards the pen.

Gail didn't raise her voice. "Cleary, stay there. He's fine."

Garcia lunged at Cleary, hit the chain-link, and fell back. Cleary didn't flinch. "Garcia, Garcia. Easy now. Easy," he said. "Gail? Get out while I have his attention."

"But—"

"Get out of there. *Now.*"

Gail slowly backed away and out of the pen.

Cleary came around and locked the gate. He grabbed Gail by her shoulders. "Don't you ever, ever go in a cage again!"

"I can do it," she said. "I can do it just as good as you."

He practically dragged her back to the trailer and shoved her inside. His hands worked and clenched. "That cat could have killed you." She steeled herself for him to hit her, but he walked out and slammed the door.

She still wore the canvas coat and gloves. She stripped them off and sat on the unmade bed. Last night, she hadn't paid much attention to the state of things inside the trailer. Last night had seemed like old times.

Nearly a year ago, Cleary had pulled a guy off Gail in a dark parking lot behind a bar on the coast, picked her up, and put her in the back of his van. She didn't know Cleary, but she was too drunk to care.

Later, in and out of fitful sleep, she would wake in a curtained-off space with one high, dirty window. Sometimes, a man sat on the side of the bed. In her dreams she heard the roar of big cats, tropical birds calling, the howl of wild dogs. The man held her hair back when she vomited, and he bathed her face. He said little. He never touched her except to help her.

She finally woke late one afternoon, alone, not knowing where she was or how long she'd been there. She made it to the toilet on her own and vomited. When she was done, she turned, wiping spittle with the back of her hand, and the man was there, leaning against the open pocket door.

"My name's Cleary," he said. "What's yours?"

When she was well enough, he took her outside and walked her around the place—a refuge for animals, he called it. All his. He had bought the place three years ago with his savings from a twenty-year stint in the postal service. "My dream ever since I was a kid," he said, "but the place has gone down. I don't know shit about what I'm doing." He used to own an ocelot and a hybrid wolf, both dead now. He'd sold a pair of lions to keep the place going. The colony of macaque monkeys was down to one female. Gail felt a deep sadness, as though she'd lost the animals, too.

Cleary bought groceries but no beer, made scrambled eggs and canned soup. "You got to eat to get strong," he would say. She had been at the refuge a couple of weeks when he asked if she had a place to go.

She thought about the dingy apartment and the guy she'd been living with, a kid, really, only twenty-two to her thirty. They'd gone to the bar together that night, but he'd done nothing to save her. Cleary had.

"No," she said. "I don't."

"Well. You could stay here."

She picked at her eggs, getting cold now. "I would need to get my car back."

"No problem," Cleary said, "if it's still there. It might not be."

He took her into town the next day. The car was where she'd left it, and she was surprised when it started. She followed Cleary back to the refuge because she didn't know the way.

Cleary worked her hard. When she put fresh hay down over the old in the petting zoo barn, he made her rake it all out, hose down the stalls, and start over. "I don't care if it's just a stall," he said. "You make one mistake, you won't learn to think, and you'll make a bigger one. You can't work that way around animals." Gail went back to the trailer most days smelling of shit. Cleary never praised her, which made her hungrier to please him. She fell into bed every night, exhausted, and he slept on the narrow couch. They moved about the claustrophobic space inside the trailer, brushing against each other, backing away, in a kind of dance. Each time she closed the sleeping alcove curtain that separated her from Cleary at night, she lay awake and heard his restless turning. One night, when Gail had been at the refuge for more than a month, she walked naked into the other room, took Cleary's hand, and led him to his own bed.

For a while, things were good. Cleary called her his little wildcat. "Just looking to be tamed, aren't you?" he would say.

When Cleary turned sullen and edgy, she got scared. She had lived this downward spiral before, but she'd thought what she had with Cleary was different.

The first time he hit her, he was headed out—the third night that week—and she stood between him and the door. "Take me with you," she said.

"I told you, no. I got business to tend to. You're not going anywhere."

"You picked up another stray, Cleary? Is that it?"

He slapped her hard and walked out. She slid down the wall and lay curled and shivering on the floor. She didn't cry.

Cleary came in at daylight and tossed a fat roll of bills on the bed. "Don't ask," he said.

That had become the pattern—Cleary going out, sometimes coming home with money, more often not, always mum about where he'd been. Gail had speculated: gambling, most likely. Or drugs. But she hadn't asked him any questions.

Now, Gail looked around the trailer that smelled of cigarettes and beer and sweat. She ran her hand over the faded sheets. She'd been a fool to come back.

Her stomach rumbled. She found half a box of stale saltines and ate all of them. She tried the door. He must have padlocked it like he did sometimes when they were both off the place, as though they had anything worth stealing. "Cleary?" She listened, yelled again. "*Cleary!* Let me out!" The tropical birds cried on the far side of the compound, in a stir about something. Garcia roared. She would know that sound anywhere.

Gail had been back a month when half a dozen guys from Alabama Wildlife and Fisheries showed up early one morning, demanding to come inside.

"I won't," Cleary said to Gail. When Cleary didn't let them in, they shattered the lock on the front gate.

"You got no right to come bustin' in here!" Cleary yelled.

One of the officers showed Cleary a badge and a handful of documents. "Complaints," he said. He told Cleary to stay out of the way until they were finished with their inspection. Cleary went for the guy, but Gail stepped between them.

"Come on," she said to Cleary. "Do what he says."

The Wildlife and Fisheries people swarmed the place. They made notes and took photographs, and when they left, they tacked a yellow paper on the front gate. "Closed until further notice," it said.

The guy with the badge gave Cleary a copy of the violations. After they were gone, Gail sat on the trailer steps and read them while Cleary paced and smoked and drank straight bourbon. Insecure cages, unsanitary conditions, inadequate food, neglect, housing dangerous animals without proper license. None of them surprised her. Cleary had been given sixty days to get the place up to code.

"Now what?" she said.

"Damned if I know." Cleary dropped his cigarette and ground it out with his boot. "You know anything about this?"

"No, I swear."

He pointed the whiskey bottle at her. "You do. You tipped 'em off, didn't you?" The half-empty bottle shattered against the trailer wall. "Goddamn it, Gail!"

She scrambled up off the steps and backed away. "It could have been anybody, Cleary. Remember the family the other day—that big woman and three bratty kids? She complained about the smell and wanted her money back. And there was a guy a couple of weeks ago, nice looking, well dressed. Didn't you think it was odd that he stopped off here? He took a lot of pictures. Remember?"

Cleary covered his face with his hands. "Yeah," he said. "I remember."

Gail was trembling. She approached him and laid her hand on his cheek. It felt sunburned, feverish. "You know I wouldn't do such a thing," she said. "I love this place."

"Shit, Gail. I know." He pulled her to him.

"We have to think about what to do," she said, her voice muffled against his chest.

He tangled his fingers in her hair and tilted her face up. "Don't worry. I'll figure something out." He let her go. He walked down the path and didn't look back.

For the next couple of weeks, they scrubbed down cages, repaired fences, picked up trash, groomed the gravel paths. Cleary set in new posts and reinforced the big cats' pens with a second layer of chain-link. Gail mowed the grassy plots, painted the picnic tables, cleaned out the petting zoo, and treated all the small animals for lice. They fell into bed at night, exhausted. There was no sex, and she was glad.

Early one afternoon, Gail heard the van leave. Cleary hadn't said anything about going out. She waited up until after midnight and finally fell asleep on the couch. Around two, Cleary stumbled in, humming a song she didn't recognize. In the dark he walked right past her to the bathroom. She heard him pee and belch. He came back and turned on the light. "You awake?"

"I am now. Where've you been?"

He popped the top on a beer and drank. "I found a way to bail us out."

Gail sat up. She had the hysterical notion that he'd robbed a bank. "What'd you do?"

He dropped beside her on the couch and kicked off his boots. He reeked of more than beer. His pupils were wide and black and bottomless. "I made a deal." He put his arm around her and whispered, "I sold Garcia."

She thought she hadn't heard him right. "You *what?*"

He slapped his thigh. "I sold the black leopard. Can you believe the luck?" He pulled a wad of cash out of his pocket and fanned the bills out on the table. "That's the deposit. A thousand bucks."

Gail got up from the couch. "We're going to breed him. He's half mine, Cleary. You can't sell him unless I say so."

Cleary knocked back the beer and tossed the can on the floor. "We can't wait around to breed him. We need money now. This guy runs a place near Tallahassee. I went to see him, showed him Garcia's papers and some photos, and he gave me the thousand on the spot, said he'll pay the rest in cash when he comes to pick him up. Three thousand dollars, Gail. *Three thousand.* He didn't bat an eye. It's enough to get us out of the hole. We can fix up the place. We can—"

"But he's *mine*, too," she said again, knowing it didn't matter.

Cleary stood, wavered, picked up the money and put it back in his jeans pocket. "I know you love that cat. Sometimes I think you love Garcia more than me." He turned her face toward the light. "That's not true, is it?"

They had never talked about love. She shook her head. "We'll make it, Gail. You'll see."

He knocked over a chair on his way to the bedroom and yanked the alcove curtain shut.

Gail rubbed her chin where Cleary had touched her. An animal moaned, long and low, somewhere in the refuge. She couldn't tell which one it was.

At dawn, she slipped out of the trailer. She loved the refuge early in the morning: light filtering through the canopy of water oaks, bougainvillea and hibiscus opening, trees alive with calling birds, not the captives but the others.

The animals that remained were a different story. Hunched at the back of his cage, the thin, mangy macaque monkey watched while she filled the water pan. The orangutan, usually feisty, didn't even rouse. The coyotes snarled and snapped. Hungry, and she had nothing to give them. Surfacing from the murky pond, the crocodile stretched his jaws. She had nothing for him, either. She spread fresh hay inside the petting zoo and threw out a few handfuls of corn, the goats nuzzling and nipping her and bedraggled chickens squawking around her feet. She didn't go in the snake house. She hated their rickety glass cages. If she'd told Cleary once, she'd told him fifty times they needed to secure the snakes or get rid of them.

But he hadn't gotten rid of the snakes and he hadn't made the refuge better and he hadn't meant it when he said he was sorry. And now he'd sold Garcia.

The cat pens were quiet. Jewel looked better. She had eaten some of yesterday's meat. Gail stayed a long time at Garcia's cage. He seemed in a kittenish mood, rolling on his back, climbing his fake tree limb and lying along its length. She wondered when the man who'd bought him would come. How much time did she and Garcia have?

She went back to the trailer. Cleary was up and calm, like he didn't remember yesterday.

"One of us needs to go to the packers'," she said. "We don't have any meat left." When they couldn't afford to order frozen meat, sometimes they bought waste cuts from a meat packing plant thirty miles away.

He took a gun out of a locked drawer. "Can't afford it. I think we can spare a goat or two. Don't you?"

Gail sat down. "Oh, Cleary, no. Don't kill them."

"I got to fix a hole in the bird enclosure," he said. "I get done with that, I'll take care of it." He held the gun out to her. "Unless you want to do it."

She looked away. "No," she said. "No."

She stayed inside the trailer and listened for the shots that came about thirty minutes later—one, then a second. Would Cleary skin the goats and butcher them? She thought not. Sometimes he went out and killed squirrels, a rabbit or two, a possum, whatever he could find, and tossed the dead animals whole into the pens. Never this.

She wondered which of the four goats he'd killed. Surely not the female.

That afternoon, she cleaned the trailer. By the time Cleary came in, she was making spaghetti. She wore a low-cut black tee and jeans. She had washed her hair and pulled it back.

He looked around. "What's this?"

He reeked of animal waste, and blood had dried on his clothes. It nauseated her, but she didn't let on. Instead, she smiled. "Go take a shower. Dinner's ready."

After dinner, while she was washing dishes, Cleary wrapped his arms around her from behind and kissed her neck. "You know," he said, "when I got this place, I thought it would be my ticket. But I screwed up. Then you came along, and I knew we could make it." He let her go. "I'll pay you back for Garcia, I swear. We'll get another cat."

"I know." She turned, and he kissed her.

"I'm going to bed," he said. "You coming?"

"Go on. I'll be there in a little while."

She waited an hour, hoping Cleary would fall asleep, but he didn't. When he pushed up the tee shirt she slept in, one of his, she didn't turn away. She lay under him and stared out the narrow window where she could see the tops of live oaks and stars and a few scudding clouds, no moon. After Cleary was done and asleep, she listened to the sounds of the night and the refuge. She imagined Garcia pacing his cage, his eyes penetrating the darkness.

It was still dark when Gail got out of bed and found the keys to the pen padlocks in Cleary's jeans. Since the day she had gone in Garcia's cage, Cleary had kept them on him. She found the money in a pocket. She took it out and peeled off a hundred. She could take more, she supposed; she could have it all, but the thought of how Cleary had gotten that money made her sick. She would take this much, to get her down the road. Cleary was welcome to the rest. She stuffed the hundred and a change of clothes in a backpack, picked up the flashlight by the door, slipped out, and made her way along the path. She looked up at the sky. No stars now.

She walked around to the back of Garcia's pen. In the flashlight's beam, his eyes glowed florescent green. He crouched, his body taut, as though he were about to spring. He would be like that in the deep woods and swamps: silent, powerful, stalking his prey, making the kill. Or would he? He'd been caged all his life. What if he ran for the highway instead? He wouldn't get far before somebody shot him.

Garcia slunk towards her, growled. "I know you're impatient," she said. "It won't be long now." She tried several keys, glancing over her shoulder, expecting not to be lucky, expecting Cleary to come.

By the time she found the right key, the sky had begun to lighten, but it was overcast, the clouds low and threatening, the air heavy with moisture. No birds called in the trees. Gail laid her palm flat against the chain-link and closed her eyes. She could hear Garcia's breathing, his footfalls on the concrete pad. It was as close to him as she would ever get. Her hands shaking, she turned the key in the padlock, wrenched it free, dropped the lock and the key ring, and opened the gate wide. She stood behind the gate and watched the cat. Garcia came to the opening, turned away. "Come on, now," she whispered. "Come out, boy." But Garcia circled the pen, rolling his head from side to side.

Gail stepped into the open. Garcia stopped and looked at her, but she didn't avert her eyes. "Come to me,

Garcia," she said, keeping her voice low. "Come to me."
And what if he came out but didn't run? What if he took
her down instead, pinned her, clamped his jaws around
her neck, dragged her into the brush? Garcia backed away,
bared his teeth, moaned. "Damn it, Garcia! Get out! Run!"
Gail picked up a piece of pipe and banged on the fence
post. Cleary might hear, but it no longer mattered. "Come
on—" A swing of the pipe— "Come *on*, come *on!* "

Birds rose out of the trees in a rush of wings like wind,
and Garcia bolted from the cage, passing so close to Gail
she might have touched him. He crossed the compound
in a zigzag pattern, and for a moment Gail lost sight of
him in a thicket of trees, but then there he was, on the
other side of the pond, gathering speed as he approached
the back fence that bordered the wilderness. He lifted
into the air in a long, graceful arc and cleared the high
fence. Gone.

She picked up her backpack and ran too, down the
path and past the trailer, expecting to see a light, or Cleary
standing in her way, but the trailer was dark. She let herself
out the private gate, locked it, got in her car and headed
down the drive and out onto the highway. She gripped the
steering wheel, her heart wild in her chest. She kept
checking the rearview mirror, but there was no sign of
Cleary.

She drove for three hours without a break. Near
Tallahassee, she stopped for gas and bought a sandwich.
Cleary might be awake by now. He might be looking for
her. He might already have reported Garcia missing. But
a cat on the loose would bring the Wildlife folks down on
him fast. It would bring out the law. She didn't think Cleary
would make the call. She felt bad for the other animals,
but it would all play out soon enough. Animal World would

shut down, and they would be rescued. That was what she told herself. What she had to believe.

She bought a map and took to the back roads, avoiding the interstate, heading south. Where she was going, she wasn't sure. She had always wanted to see the Everglades. Now was as good a time as any, but it was a long, long way. She had sixty dollars left. Tonight, she would sleep in the car. Tomorrow, she would need to find some godforsaken, one-stoplight town and stay a while, get a job waitressing or tending bar, hunker down in case Cleary came looking. Then she would move on, like she'd always done.

The day had turned clear and hot. Garcia would be miles and miles from the refuge by now, running at a steady pace as though he knew where he was headed, going deeper into the wilderness until it swallowed him up. She willed him to be safe. She willed him a better place.

PIECES

1.

Barbara thinks the model airplane, a P-38 Lightning, is too complicated for Josh, but it's his eleventh birthday and his money. Steven watches, his chin resting on his crossed arms. Steven is seven, a pest. When he picks up a frame and twists off a part, Josh slaps his hand.

"You touch that again and you're dead," Josh says.

"Am not," Steven says.

Barbara sighs. "All right, you two. One more outburst and you go straight to bed."

It has taken Josh and Barbara half an hour to snap the plastic pieces from their frames. Barbara finds the empty frames themselves interesting—their odd spaces, sticks that go nowhere, knobs with rough edges where the pieces have broken off.

Tiny plastic parts coded in order of assembly cover the kitchen table: the A parts in a pile, then B, then C, and on and on. Barbara reads the directions again. Words like fuselage, twin engine booms, tail assembly. The model cement fumes are giving her a headache.

Josh hands her the engine boom he's just glued together. "This one's done," he says. "Check it out."

She gets cement on her hands. "It's messy, Josh." She cleans the seams with a Q-tip dipped in nail polish remover and gives it back to him. "Don't use quite so much."

"I *know*, Mom," he says. And he does. More than a dozen model planes fill the shelves in his room, models he's finished with little help from either Sam or her. He can tell you the names of the planes, their specs, when and where they were built, how they functioned in whatever war. This is the first one that's frustrated him. She's sorry she let him buy it.

Josh struggles to fit the propeller on the second engine. "It won't go," he says.

Barbara pushes the diagrams toward him. "Follow the directions."

He sighs and rolls his eyes, that sappy, preadolescent thing he's started lately.

She peels the cement off her fingers like a layer of skin. She wishes Sam were home. Her shoulders hurt. She gets up, stretches, rubs the back of her neck, walks around the table. They've been at this for two hours. "Let's stop for now," she says. "You can work on it tomorrow. Your dad'll be home. He can help."

Josh scrapes his chair back hard. "I wouldn't bet on it," he says. He stalks off to his room.

2.

A gray morning on St. George Island. Low, threatening clouds, slate water, a blending of sky and Gulf except where the waves build far out and heave themselves at the shore, pound away at the beach and leave a sharp ledge where there should be hard, smooth slopes of sand. Today there are only broken shells, loops and tangles of seaweed, driftwood, debris.

Tire tracks on the sand. The beach patrol has come by early and posted red warning flags that whip in the wind like flames. Gulls halt and hover, treading wind like water, then surrender and settle in flocks and huddle close. Most days you can see the shallows and the deeps, know where to wade or swim, ride the waves on plastic floats, take out the Sunfish. But on days like this, the Gulf hides currents strong enough to pull a grown man under, sap his strength, and drag him out to sea.

3.

The day that Len drowns in the Gulf off St. George Island, Sam calls Barbara from the office. "Something bad happened," he says. "I'm on my way home."

"What do you mean, something bad?"

The words catch in his throat. "It's Len. Len is dead."

"He's *what?*"

"This morning. He drowned." Sam waits for Barbara to say something, but all he hears is her breathing. "Holly's brother is driving her and Charlie and Evan back. They're supposed to be home around eight. We need to go over there, so get a sitter."

"Oh, Sam. I'm so sorry," Barbara says.

"Yeah. Me too." He hangs up.

Sam knows exactly what time Holly called. He had just looked at his watch and thought good, eleven-thirty, another thirty minutes and he could get out of the office, go work out for half an hour, grab a quick bite.

Holly had sounded so calm. "Len drowned, Sam," she'd said. No "I have something terrible to tell you," just straight out. She might as well have said, "Len hit a hole-in-one," or "Len caught a six-foot shark." She told Sam they hadn't found his body yet.

Sam's stomach cramped. He asked Holly if there was anything he could do. What a lame thing to say, but he said it.

"No," she'd said. "There's nothing anybody can do."

After they hung up, Sam had gone in the bathroom and vomited. Then he'd called Barbara.

He doesn't go home right away. He sits at his desk and clenches his fists to keep his hands from shaking, and he thinks about Len. Len was a superman, good at everything. A terrific athlete, a great swimmer. Len was his best friend. How could he drown?

Sam wonders if Len had known what was happening. He wonders what it feels like to be dragged under and down and out to sea and fight it and not win. Sam doesn't pray often, but he finds himself praying that Len had a heart attack, an aneurysm, something, anything besides gulping in water instead of air, that Len hadn't known he was drowning.

4.

The two couples had taken their last beach trip together the summer before.

Barbara wasn't a good swimmer, and even though Josh and Steven were, she wouldn't let them near the surf or the pool unless either she or Sam was with them. But Holly worked on her tan. Her boys ran wild, from the pool to the beach and back, all over the place. When Len talked Sam into going for a long swim in the surf, Barbara stood on the wet shelf of sand and watched them swim out of sight. She waited there until they came jogging back down the beach.

One morning, Len rented a Jet Ski and took his boys out. When Josh and Steven begged to go, Barbara said they couldn't, but Sam overruled her. Barbara sat in the shallow water, her knees drawn up, her arms wrapped around them. The Jet Ski ripped through the water, slapped the tops of the waves, threw up a plume of spray. Josh and Steven took turns riding behind Len, holding on to him, waving and yelling each time they passed by. Sam and Holly yelled back. Barbara didn't.

The last day, Len insisted that he teach Barbara and Sam and the two older boys drown-proofing. "It's something everybody should know," he said. "Rip currents are treacherous."

Barbara tried to beg off. Somebody had to watch the younger boys, she said. Evan was four, Steven six then.

"I'll keep an eye on them," Holly said. "Go, Barbara. I know about drown-proofing. Len already taught me." Holly lowered her sunglasses and smiled at Len. So Barbara, feeling humiliated, took a kickboard and swam out with Sam, Len, Josh, and Charlie.

The Gulf was almost glassy smooth that day, but Len showed them how to swim as if there were a riptide. "Watch out for deep, dark, choppy water," he yelled. "The main thing is, don't panic." He was treading water effortlessly. "Relax. Let the current carry you. It'll take you out for a while, but then, it'll diverge and weaken. All you have to do is swim with the tide, whatever direction it goes. It may take a while, but eventually, you'll swim out of it."

Barbara quickly had enough and started paddling back toward the beach, but Len stopped her and swung her kickboard around. "Come on, Barbara. Pretend I'm a riptide," he said. He was grinning. He held on to the front of the board and pulled her along.

"Stop, Len," she said, but he kept swimming a strong sidestroke, pulling her fast, the swells slapping her face.

"Hey, Barb, way to go!" Len said. She hated being called Barb. Surely he knew that.

Sam shouted, "Don't, Len! She's scared."

Len let go of the board, slung his wet hair back out of his eyes, and looked at Sam. "Okay, sure. Sorry," he said. He swam away, a ferocious, competitive, Australian crawl.

Sam was beside Barbara then, and Josh and Charlie, too. "You okay?" Sam said. Breathless, she nodded. She was shivering. They swam with her back to the beach.

Holly was stretched out face down on a towel. Steven and Evan were way down the beach, sitting on the sand where the waves barely lapped at them.

Len apologized to Barbara later, but she and Sam argued fiercely when they got home from that trip. She would not go with Len and Holly again, not ever.

5.

Holly had slept in. She wasn't on the beach. She didn't see what happened. Charlie saw, but he wouldn't talk about it. All Holly knew was what other people told her.

6.

Sam had often wondered what it would be like to do the things Len did: ride a motorcycle, go mountain climbing or skydiving, give up a six-figure law practice and take a job as a public defender. Holly never seemed to mind when Len did something risky. On the contrary, she seemed proud. "Did you hear what Len did?" she would say, looking at him like she could eat him up.

The closest Sam had come to doing something daring was the summer years ago when the two couples had gone to Belize. "It's paradise," Len had said. "You won't regret it."

Len and Holly were certified to dive, but Sam needed to take a class.

Barbara balked when he asked her to take the class with him. "You know I'm not a good enough swimmer, Sam," she said, but she pouted for days when he signed up without her.

He talked her into going on the trip anyway. The dives would take only part of the day, he told her. They would have lots of time together. But things were sour from the beginning. Josh was only a year old, and Barbara was homesick for him. She went out on the boat, but she wouldn't go in the water, not even to snorkel. Sam knew she didn't want him going in either, but he did. He would never forget that first time: shafts of sunlight filtering down, fish swimming right up to your face mask, the colors in the reef. It felt ethereal, disconnected from the real world.

That night, he begged Barbara to try snorkeling. "It's so beautiful," he said. "I'll be right there with you. You'll be fine."

"I can't, Sam. Please let me stay here tomorrow. I'd love to lie on the beach and read and get some sun. I'll call and check on Josh."

"I don't want to go without you," he said.

"I really don't mind if you go. I don't want to spoil it for you."

In Sam's mind, she'd spoiled it already.

The next day, Barbara stayed behind while Sam and Len and Holly went out again. Holly was something to see in a wet suit that left nothing to the imagination, jumping off the side of the boat, squealing like a kid. Underwater, she was luminous in the refracted light, her movements as smooth and sensuous as a fish. Sam thought of mermaids.

Len announced at dinner that night that he'd set up a night dive. "You in, Sam?"

Sam glanced at Barbara. "Yeah, I guess. Sounds like

fun."

Barbara tossed her napkin on the table. "You can't be serious, Sam." She got up and walked away, and Sam followed her.

"Apron strings a little short, are they, my friend?" Len said, laughing.

Sam had not gone scuba diving since, even though Len had invited him a few times to go with a group of men. Sam resented the hell out of it, although he knew it wasn't really Barbara's fault that he wasn't more like Len. That he wasn't man enough to stand up to her.

7.

Evan went out in the surf after his daddy told him not to. A big wave knocked Evan down. He went under. He was scared. He was making air bubbles under the water. His daddy rescued him. His daddy was the greatest superhero in the whole world.

8.

After their last trip to the beach with Len and Holly, it dawned on Barbara that she needn't be jealous of Holly. Len was far more likely to lure Sam away from her with his escapades, his bravado. She could see the yearning in Sam's eyes when he listened to Len's stories about his elk hunt or the last scuba diving trip or the homeless guy he'd gotten acquitted on a robbery charge. She wouldn't be surprised, even as much as Len and Holly seemed to love each other, if Len had had an affair. Yes. It was Len Barbara should be afraid of.

When Len died, Barbara was ashamed that the first thing she felt was relief.

9.

When Sam and Barbara got to Holly's house—now Holly's, Barbara reminded herself, not Len's—she wasn't home yet. A dozen other friends had already gathered. They all shook their heads. Len was a strong swimmer. Unbelievable.

The kitchen was filling up with casseroles, fried chicken, pound cakes, meat trays from the supermarket deli.

Margaret, Holly's next-door neighbor, whispered to Barbara, "Their bed's unmade. Do you think I should make it up?" Margaret had tears in her eyes. "I wouldn't want people traipsing all over my house, noticing things undone."

Barbara said, "I think Holly would appreciate it, Margaret."

Margaret nodded. She looked relieved. She headed down the hall to the bedroom.

A big, expensive black and white photo hung over the mantel. Holly, Len, and the boys, sitting on a dune, sea oats swaying behind them, the Gulf in the background, waves breaking. Holly beautiful in a white strapless sundress, her long blonde hair loose and windswept. Len wearing white linen slacks and a white shirt with the sleeves rolled, the boys in white shorts and shirts. They were all smiling, looking straight at the camera. What a good-looking family they were. Perfect, you might say.

10.

Sam lies awake nights. If he had been there, could he have saved him?

11.

Holly, Charlie, and Evan show up at Barbara and Sam's

about five-thirty on a Wednesday afternoon. "Is Sam here?" Holly holds out a brown envelope. "Insurance. I can't make any sense out of it. I hope Sam can help."

"He's not home yet."

Holly says, "I'd like to wait for him, if it's okay. Are your boys here?"

"They're upstairs," Barbara says.

Holly says to her kids, "They're here. Go on up."

Evan pushes past Barbara and thunders up the stairs, yelling for Steven. Charlie doesn't move.

Holly says, "Charlie, go on. Keep an eye on Evan for me."

Charlie, dragging his feet, hands shoved deep in the pockets of his baggy shorts, comes up the steps onto the porch.

Barbara holds the door open. "Hey, Charlie," she says. He passes her without a word and trudges up the stairs.

Holly follows him inside. "Sorry. He's like that sometimes."

Barbara gives Holly a Diet Coke and they sit at the kitchen table covered with model parts. "Excuse the mess," Barbara says.

Holly says, "You should see my place."

There's an awkward silence. Barbara hasn't seen Holly since the funeral two weeks ago. Finally, she says, "How are you, Holly?"

Holly shrugs. "We're okay." She looks away then, shakes her head. "Well, you see how Charlie is. Evan wakes up nights, screaming. To tell you the truth, they're driving me crazy." She smiles, but not like the old Holly. The flirty tilt of her head, the flutter of eyelashes gone. "I guess that's hard for you to understand."

Barbara runs her finger down the cold condensation on the Coke can. "Yeah, I guess it is." She looks up. "Holly, they're what you have left of Len."

"I know. That's the crazy part. I can hardly stand to

look at them, they remind me so much of him." She's crying, and Barbara wonders if she should touch her. Hug her. Something. She gets up and hands Holly a Kleenex.

12.

Charlie saw it all. Or did he dream it?

His dad pointed to the red flags, walked knee-deep into the water and drew an imaginary line. "You can come this far," he said. "No farther. Got it?"

His dad settled in a beach chair with a book. Charlie walked along the beach where the water broke into foam. He watched the little shells they called angelwings bury themselves in the sand. The breakers were huge. No way he was going into that. Then he saw his brother moving out into the surf. "Dad!" he yelled, "Evan's gone past the line!"

Without looking up from the book, their dad yelled, "Come back, Evan!" But Evan didn't come back. A wave knocked him down and before he could stand up, another one took him under. He came up sputtering, yelled "Daddy!" and went under again. Their dad ran into the surf and lunged toward where Evan had been, but Evan came up gasping and crying maybe ten yards farther out.

Charlie watched their dad swim against the breakers toward Evan, reach him, and grab him. Then he was swimming toward the shore like a lifeguard, carrying Evan. Charlie waded out waist-deep, rode the waves and fought to keep his balance, the tide sucking at his legs, the bottom shifting away under his feet. When their dad got within a few yards of Charlie, he yelled, "Stay where you are!" Then he lifted Evan out of the water and pushed him toward Charlie on the crest of a wave. Charlie reached for Evan and caught hold of his arm just as a wave broke over them and knocked them down. Charlie struggled up and somehow held on to Evan and dragged him to the shallows. He turned to look for his dad and spotted him out beyond the breakers, his strong strokes cutting through the water, but *oh shit* he was swimming sideways, the way he'd taught Charlie to do last summer. Then he lost sight of him in the swells.

Charlie stood knee-deep in waves battering his legs. He was still gripping Evan's arm when a man grabbed both of them and pulled them out of the water. "Are y'all crazy?" the man yelled. "Didn't you see the damn flags?"

13.

Barbara walks in the den. Sam and Holly are sitting on the couch, papers spread out on the coffee table. Holly laughs. "Oh, *Sam*," she says.

"Hey," Barbara says.

Sam and Holly look up. Sam's grin fades. "Hey. What is it, Barbara?" he says, one eyebrow raised in that way he has, half amused, half not.

She pastes on a smile. "Holly, I thought you and the boys might like to stay for supper. There's plenty."

Before Holly can answer, Barbara hears yelling and the sound of something shattering in the front hall. Footsteps overhead, what sounds like a scuffle.

"Mom!" Josh yells. "Evan's tearing up my planes!"

By the time Barbara gets to the front hall, three of Josh's model airplanes lie broken on the slate floor. Another one whizzes past her head and breaks apart at her feet. She looks up at Evan, hanging over the banister at the top of the stairs, a model plane in each hand. Josh is trying to wrestle them away from him.

"Evan, *no*," she says.

Evan elbows Josh in the stomach, Josh lets go, and

Evan, grinning, sails the planes off the landing and makes a high-pitched *sheeeee* sound as they fall. Barbara starts up the stairs, but Charlie has already pulled his brother off the banister and he's punching him.

"*Stop* it!" Charlie yells. "*Stop* it, Evan!" Evan covers his head with his arms and howls.

Sam and Holly are in the hall, too. Holly yells at Charlie to leave Evan alone, but Charlie has Evan on the floor, still hitting him. Sam passes Barbara on the stairs and reaches the top in three strides. He separates Charlie and Evan, and Charlie pounds Sam's chest now, but Sam doesn't let him go. He holds him tight until the hitting stops. Josh and Steven lean over the banister, looking down at the wreckage of Josh's planes. Josh wipes his eyes on his sleeve.

Barbara hears Holly's choked sob. Holly stands at the foot of the stairs, one hand over her mouth, her pretty face mottled red, tears streaming down, and Barbara wonders if this is how it feels to lose control, to fight the current the way Len must have, to hold your breath until you can't hold it any longer.

Barbara goes down the stairs. "Come on, Holly," she says. "Let Sam handle it." She looks back up at Sam, sitting on the top step with Charlie on one side and Evan on the other, his arms around both of them, and Barbara feels something give way deep inside her. It's almost audible, like a shell breaking.

She puts her arm around Holly and takes her to the kitchen. "Here, sit," she says. She gives her a fresh tissue and takes one for herself. Barbara can hear the murmur of Sam's calm voice. She takes a deep breath and asks Holly again to stay, hoping, dear God, she'll say no.

"No, thanks," Holly says. "I can't, not after—" She glances toward the hall. "I need to take them home." She looks at her watch, then at Barbara. "This is the hardest time, you know?"

Barbara doesn't know. She doesn't understand what
Holly means—the time of day, or the time of grief? She
nods anyway.

Holly says, "I'm so sorry, Barbara. Tell Josh I'll replace
his planes."

"Don't worry about it."

Barbara doesn't tell her how long it took Josh to build
those planes, how special they were. Later that night, she'll
tell Josh that model planes are just things. He can buy and
build new ones. What she won't say is, once you lose a father,
you never get him back.

A few minutes later, Sam comes into the kitchen, one
arm around Charlie and holding Evan's hand. Neither of
the boys looks up.

Holly says, "Thanks, Sam," and then, like an afterthought,
"you too, Barbara."

Barbara can't find any words.

Sam gives both boys a hug. "No problem," he says.

Holly gets her purse and the insurance papers from
the den. Barbara and Sam stand on the porch and watch
Holly and the boys go down the walk, get in her SUV,
and drive away.

When they go inside, Steven is sitting on the stairs. Josh is
on his knees in the midst of the shattered planes. Barbara stoops
and begins to pick up bits and pieces of plastic. Broken fuselage,
wings, engines, propellers, rudders, tiny plastic men.

THE TASTE OF SALT

Abby first noticed her hair falling out in the shower. She gathered up a handful so it wouldn't clog the drain. What was she going to do—save it? She sat on the shower floor and cried. Her doctor, her oncology counselor, and her support group had told her to expect the hair loss.

Eric knocked on the bathroom door. "Abby? You okay?"

"Yeah. I'll be out in a minute."

She got the scissors and chopped her long hair off in chunks. She tried to imagine a pixie cut, an Audrey Hepburn do. When she finished, she blew it dry. She looked at the back and sides with a hand mirror. Ragged. She would have to go to her hairdresser, confess she had cut it herself, and get it evened up. But what was the use? She would probably lose it all anyway.

When she came out of the bathroom, Eric was in bed, reading. He looked up. "You cut it. It looks good."

She shook her head. "It looks awful. It's all coming out."

He put his book down. "Come here."

She switched off the light on her side of the bed and slipped under the covers. Every night, Eric kissed her cheek or her hair, said goodnight, told her he loved her. Most nights, he held her hand until she went to sleep.

Tonight, he rubbed her back. "Feel good?"

"Hmm, yes." Her muscles stayed tight, like the clutch in her gut that was always there. He switched off his lamp and snuggled against her, kneading her shoulders. He turned her toward him and kissed her, his hand trailing down her stomach, her thighs. She stiffened. Was he avoiding her breasts? Her breast, she corrected herself.

"Abby, please. Keep your gown on if you want to."

"Not tonight, Eric. Soon."

His hand was still. "I love you. The breast doesn't matter."

"It matters to me," she said. "It matters a lot."

He sighed and rolled away from her. Abby stared at the skylight over the bed. A full moon. "I've been thinking," she said into the dark, "I'd be happy if you remarried. I expect you to when something happens to me."

"Don't say things like that," Eric said.

"No, really. I want you to go out and have fun. Go dancing. You always loved to dance and I didn't. Find yourself a good dancer."

He threw the covers back and sat up. "This is crazy. Would you stop?"

"You could have a child. You're not too old." But I am, she thought. Too old. Too sick.

"Jesus, Abby. Didn't we settle that a long time ago? I don't need a kid. I need you." He got out of bed without turning on the light and pulled on his jeans. "I can't listen to this anymore." He went to the closet and grabbed a shirt, picked up his keys off the bedside table and walked out.

"Where are you going?"

"For a walk. I'll be back in a little while."

She heard his footsteps on the stairs, the back door slamming. She rolled over onto his side of the bed, still warm. What was wrong with her, goading him that way?

Eric had gone with her to the oncologist the day she got the diagnosis: stage III breast cancer with some involvement of the chest wall, a couple of positive nodes. Eric hadn't let go of her hand while the doctor talked about surgery, chemo options, survival rates. Percentages. Her life, reduced to numbers. She didn't look at Eric, not once. Even now, she couldn't bear the helpless look in his eyes when she caught him with his guard down, looking at her.

She was alone in the house except for the cat, Miso, a part-Siamese male she'd found after a thunderstorm nine years ago. Abby and Eric had gone out to dinner and a movie. It had stormed earlier, one of those big, booming thunderstorms with a dramatic lightning show. As Eric was unlocking the back door, she stopped him. "Wait," she said. "Listen."

"What?"

"I thought I heard a kitten."

Eric cocked his head. "I don't hear anything."

"There it is again. Hear it?" Abby got a flashlight and walked down the driveway, calling. "Kitty? Here, kitty. Kitty, kitty, kitty?" She found the cat huddled under the shrubbery next to the house. She picked it up. "Poor little thing. It's shivering," she said.

Inside, she got an old towel and dried the kitten off. It looked to be six, maybe eight weeks old. Little. Where was its mother? Abby was angry that somebody had put it out on the street. She gave it a saucer of milk and put it in a cardboard box. She put up signs in the neighborhood, but nobody claimed it. All week, the thought of taking the kitten to the shelter plagued Abby. What if nobody wanted him?

The day they'd planned to take him, Eric said, "I know you want to keep him."

"I'd like to," she said. "I like holding him. He's sweet."

She named him Miso because they'd gone for sushi the night she found him. Miso was a one-person cat. He allowed Eric to feed him, but that was all. Until her surgery, Miso hadn't let anybody except Abby touch him. Since the day she came home from the hospital, the cat had refused to come near her.

The cat prowled the house, meowing, like he was lost again. She willed Eric to come home. He did, finally, at one in the morning. When he came to bed, she reached for him. "I'll try harder," she said.

"I hope so," Eric said. "I really do."

Morning. Miso lay behind the couch. The woman called his name. "Miso? Where are you? Come out, Miso. Kitty kitty kitty." Her footsteps going away. The sick smell of the woman made him think of his crate, of cages and hands, not the woman's, but rough hands holding him on a cold table, needles, pain. The man called him too and rattled the food in his bowl, but still Miso hid. He didn't like the man. It was the woman Miso wanted.

He came out after the moon rose, awake and watching in the night, and when the moon set, he slept and dreamed and in the dream the sickness smell was gone. He rubbed against the woman's legs and jumped in her lap, arching his back against her hand that stroked him in the rhythm of his purr.

After the next round of chemo, Abby's best friend, Sarah, came and brought daffodils, homemade vegetable soup

Abby didn't feel like eating, and a silk scarf, hand-painted
with abstract swaths of deep blues and greens. Sarah folded
it into a triangle, made another fold, wrapped it around
Abby's head, tied it, and tucked the ends. "Not bad," Sarah
said. "Want to see?"

Abby shook her head.

"Come on, Abby, it looks good. It's very striking."

Abby pulled the scarf off. "Take it back, Sarah. Please."

Sarah sat down. "I'm trying to help you. Let me help."

Abby looked away, the scarf dangling in her hand.

"Fine, I'll return it. But they say scarves are more
comfortable than a wig."

Abby often heard *they say* from well-meaning friends,
none of whom had had a breast cut off or had been
pumped full of poison to try to make the cancer go away.

Sarah walked over to the piano. "Are you playing now?"

"No." She hadn't played since the day she got the
diagnosis.

"You should," Sarah said. "It would do you good to get
back to it."

Abby had heard *should* a lot, too. "I'm really tired. I
need to lie down."

"Okay," Sarah said. "I'll go. Call me if you need
anything."

After Sarah left, Abby brushed her hand over the dusty
piano keys. For nine years after she graduated from Oberlin,
Abby had made guest appearances with symphony
orchestras all over the country. She was that good. Eric had
walked up to her after a concert one night in New Orleans,
that lock of hair falling over his eyebrow, his green eyes, his
face serious. He said, "I'm going to marry you." She laughed.
A year later, they did marry, and the concert life, the travel,
began to wear her down. She missed Eric, and they wanted
a child. She gave up touring to try to have a baby, but it

didn't happen. There were miscarriages, then fertility treatments. Sex became a chore. When the fertility treatments failed, they decided against adoption. It wouldn't be the end of the world to be a childless couple. They had each other. Eric threw himself into his law practice and volunteered as a Big Brother. Even though Abby had given up performing as a concert artist, she still had her music.

She performed with the local chamber orchestra, gave piano lessons, and accompanied the choir at their Episcopal church. Until the diagnosis, music had run through her head, unbidden. She'd sometimes catch herself humming a classical melody aloud in the grocery store where people looked at her like she was crazy. At home she'd play for hours, lost in the music, while Miso lay in a slant of sun under the piano, his blue eyes half closed as though he were listening.

After her diagnosis, Abby had shut out the music.

"Play for me," Eric would say.

"I can't. I just can't."

Music had always made her feel hopeful. She couldn't afford to feel hopeful now. She couldn't tolerate that vulnerability or invest anything in this world until she heard the word *remission*.

Miso sat under the piano and meowed, looking forlorn. He missed the sounds the woman used to make there, bigger than a yard full of birds, bigger than the loudest wind. He scratched and licked himself. He wanted to curl against the woman's warm chest and feel the thrum that almost matched his own, but the smell of her frightened him, like thunder or the black dog he sometimes saw in the yard, beyond the glass, out in the world where he couldn't go.

Abby saw herself in the mirror one morning when she got out of the shower: thin, her right breast full, beginning to droop a little, the red line of scar where the left breast had been, her swollen left arm. She cupped her right breast and her left hand shaped a ghost of the other. She ran her finger along the scar but felt nothing. The surgeon had said the numbness would go away in time, but numbness seemed appropriate, as though part of her was dead.

She fiercely guarded the scar from Eric, always undressing and dressing in the bathroom with the door closed. One day, he walked in on her. She grabbed a towel and covered herself. Miso lay outside the door, his ears back, tail twitching.

"What are you doing, Eric? You can't just walk in here." She backed away.

"I used to. You didn't seem to mind."

"I didn't, before."

"Let me see the scar, Abby. Don't shut me out like this." Eric's hands closed over hers.

"I don't want you looking at me."

"Please."

"I said *no*. I'm not ready."

He let go. "All right. If that's what you want."

He went out and closed the door. Abby heard him say, "Move out of the way, Miso!" Then the cat's yowl and his skittering feet on the wood floors. She sat on the side of the tub. Why wouldn't Eric leave her alone? That was all she wanted. Or was it?

By the time she came out of the bathroom, he had left the house.

When she told Sarah what had happened, Sarah didn't say anything. "What?" Abby said. "What are you thinking?"

"You won't like it," Sarah said. She reached for Abby's hands and held them. "Eric has been so good and patient.

None of this is his fault." Sarah shook her head. "Keep this up, and you'll drive him away."

Abby started to cry. "You think I don't know that? Wouldn't he be better off?"

They were sitting at Abby's kitchen table. Sarah got up and wrapped Abby in her arms. "You aren't going to die. I won't let you. Neither will Eric."

Voices of the woman and the man, hushed like wind or high like birds, thunder of footsteps in and out the door, gusts of cold air. Once, Miso bolted for the open and the man yelled at him, Get back here! Miso crawled behind the couch. After the man yelled at the woman, after he had gone, Miso heard the woman's voice, not speaking, but the sound she made when he licked the water from her face that tasted like salt. The cat liked salt. He came out from behind the couch and looked for the woman, but there were many doors and they were all closed.

When the nausea subsided after the last chemo treatment, Abby told Eric she was going to the mall. He put down the newspaper. "That's great," he said. "I'll go with you."

"You don't need to."

"We could get some lunch. You okay?"

"Sure, I'm fine."

How many times in the last months had he asked her that? She dressed and put on the blue hat Sarah had knitted for her.

She insisted he drop her near the mall's east entrance. "Don't try to find me. I'll call you when I'm done."

The automatic doors slid open, then closed. She wondered if Eric was sitting in the car, watching. The wig shop was on the second floor. She walked past it several times before she could bring herself to go inside. It looked classy, not what she expected. Soft music played, and an older saleswoman with large breasts put her in a tiny private room. Were the woman's breasts real, or had she had surgery, too? When Abby took the hat off, exposing her nearly bald scalp, the woman didn't look away.

"My name's Rita," the woman said. She asked Abby about her family.

"No children. My husband and I—we have a cat. Siamese."

Rita asked Abby what her natural hair color was, and when Abby said drab, Rita laughed.

She brought Abby dark brown wigs, everything from pixie cuts to vampish curls. Between wigs Abby closed her eyes. She tried on at least a dozen. "I don't think this is going to work," she said.

"Oh, we're not done yet," Rita said. She brought out more: blond wigs, lighter shades of brown, even red. Abby began to feel sick.

"How about this one?" Rita fitted another on Abby's head. "Look how pretty you are."

Abby opened her eyes. The image in the mirror had her thin face, her dark brown eyes, and a chin-length auburn bob with bangs.

"Touch the hair, play with it," Rita said.

When Abby tossed her head, the hair moved naturally. The wig didn't feel tight or heavy. Then Abby thought, no. She said, "I don't think so. It doesn't look like me."

"It suits you," Rita said. "Try it. You can always bring it back."

When the woman was away, Miso ambled through the house. The sick smell was fainter now. Sometimes, if the piano was open, he walked across the keys. He crept into the bathroom, sniffed a strand of the woman's hair on

the floor, and bolted back through the bedroom and down
the hall to the den where he returned to his place behind
the couch, his ears flattened, his teeth bared. He lay alert
and listened for the woman. At last his brain told him
food, told him water, told him sleep. Told him forget, and
for the moment, the woman was forgotten.

Abby came out of the wig store and spotted Eric sitting
on a bench. He must have guessed where she'd gone. She
walked toward him, and he whistled.

"Wow," he said. "Look at you."

She wanted to snatch the wig off. She felt like a fraud.
She remembered a woman in her cancer support group,
Margaret, who had died—her shaved head, her bold eyes
and radiant smile. Abby wished she were that brave. Abby
said, "This is crazy. I'm taking it back."

"No. Keep it. You look gorgeous." He kissed her cheek.
"Come on. Let's grab some lunch, if you feel like it. You
feel like it, don't you?"

A wave of nausea swept over her. "Sure."

At the restaurant Abby ordered tomato bisque, the
mildest thing on the menu.

"Is that all you're going to have?" Eric said. "You need
to eat."

"I'm not very hungry." She put down her spoon, sipped
water.

Eric said, "Are you okay?"

"I told you, Eric. I'm fine."

"I don't think you are. Want to tell me what's wrong?"

She set her glass down a little too hard. How could he
not know? "Okay. You want to know what's wrong? I feel
sick. I'm scared. I don't want to die."

Eric leaned forward in his chair. "I know you're scared,
sweetheart. I understand that. I'm scared, too. But you've

got this—this *wall* around you, and you won't let me in. You won't even let me touch you." His voice choked with tears. "Sometimes, I feel like you've already left me, Abby. Like you don't really want to live."

"Oh, Eric. Stop."

He wiped his eyes with the back of his hand. He waved the waitress over, got the check, and slapped a couple of twenties down. "Let's go," he said.

They didn't speak all the way home. Eric dropped Abby off and went to his law office. "Just for a couple of hours," he said.

"On Saturday? You never go in on Saturday."

"Yeah. Got some catching up to do."

Abby watched him drive away. "I'm sorry," she said to the car disappearing around the corner. "I'm so sorry."

She went inside. Her footsteps echoed on the polished wood floors. Miso lay on the den floor in a spot of sunlight. He didn't bolt when she entered the room. A good sign, she thought. She walked through the living room, past the piano. Its cold silence mocked her.

Keep this up, and you'll drive him away, Sarah had said. If she lost Eric, she would lose everything.

The woman lay on the couch. Miso crept near her face and smelled her breath, sweeter now, like the milk she sometimes gave him. He curled against her. A hummingbird darted at the door made of glass. Long ago, when he was allowed to live in the outside world, he had stalked and caught and brought birds to the door for the woman to find. She'd said, No Miso, no killing. He had liked the taste of bird's blood, the way bones cracked between his jaws, but they had brought him into the house and kept him there. No more going outside, no more birds.

The woman opened her eyes. "You're here, Miso! Oh, I've missed you." She scratched his head, and his purr began. He let her touch until a sound startled him and he leapt off the couch. The woman got up and spoke into the thing she held in her hand. She was talking to some other, not to him.

Eric came home around five. They ate in silence, and afterwards, they watched television, Eric with the remote in his hand, flipping channels. At ten, he said, "I'm going to bed."

"Okay. I'll be there in a little while."

She turned off the TV and the lamp and sat in the dark. After a while, she got up, went upstairs, and took a shower. By the time she came out of the bathroom, Eric's light was still on, but his eyes were closed. A book lay face down on his chest.

She got into bed. "Hey," she said. "You awake?" She closed the book and put it on her bedside table.

"I am now."

She stripped off her gown and lay down beside him. "Abby," he said. She closed her eyes while he traced the scar with his finger. He kissed it, light kisses she could barely feel all along the line of it, and then he drew her to him and held her. She held tight to him. The cat scratched at their bedroom door, wanting to be let in.

Miso jumped up on the wide windowsill and looked out. One small bird was there, but then there were two, then one, then many, a blurring of birds and trees, sky and world turning. He rubbed his face with his paws, jumped down to the floor, but it heaved and tilted so he had trouble standing. He lay down and waited for the floor to right itself. After a while, it did.

When the woman put out food, Miso backed away. She said, "What's the matter, Miso? You don't like it?" He went behind the couch and didn't come out when she called. He wanted to, but the trickery of the floor had frightened him. Better to stay in the corner where it was dark and quiet and still.

Abby's hair grew in white and curly. She abandoned the wig. Six months post-op, Eric went with her for her follow-up MRI. She waited two days for the doctor's office to call. When Abby saw the clinic name on the caller ID, she let the phone ring. Eric answered and handed it to her. She took a deep breath, listened, said, "Yes, thank you. I understand." She hung up.

"Well?" Eric said. He had gone pale.

"The MRI is clean," she said. "I'm in remission. Can you believe it?" Abby didn't say that the nurse had told her to come back in three months for another scan. She started to cry. She let Eric hold her. She felt his fast heartbeat, heard his breath catch. When she stepped away, he brushed her tears away with his thumb. She brushed away his.

"All right," he said. He smiled. "Let's celebrate."

"Not yet. When it's been a year, maybe."

"No. Let's do it now."

She looked away. "Why? You think I won't make it a year?"

"Jesus, Abby. No. It's not that at all. Let's start living, okay? Let's go to New Orleans, just for a weekend."

"We can talk about it," she said.

He put a finger to her lips. "No talking. We're going."

The night before they were supposed to leave, Abby said, "I'm worried about the cat. He's not eating. Something's not right. Maybe we should take him to the vet."

"He'll be fine," Eric said. "Don't worry so much."

~ ~ ~

Their first afternoon in the French Quarter, Eric pulled her into a lingerie shop on Bourbon Street. The place looked like a bordello—tall, ornately carved oak doors, red brocade walls, low lights, mannequins in provocative poses. Eric bought her a black silk nightgown that looked like an evening gown out of a 1940s movie, wide straps, a little covered up, which she liked. She'd never owned such a thing. She felt silly when she put it on but very much alive. When they made love, they were gentle and fierce by turns, like new lovers.

When they got home, Miso was throwing up and lethargic. The vet kept him for days, ran tests, and found an inoperable tumor the size of a half dollar at the base of Miso's brain. The vet was a friend. He knew about Abby's cancer. He looked glum.

"We should put Miso down," he said. "Otherwise, you're looking at a slow, painful decline."

"Like what?" Abby asked.

The vet shook his head. "Three months, I'd guess. Maybe less. It's hard to say. He'll go blind. He'll lose his functions. He'll have seizures."

Abby said, "I can take care of him."

She told Eric that night what the vet had said and what she intended to do. "You can't," he said.

"I can. I will. What if the vet is wrong? I can't give up on Miso. Not yet."

For the next few weeks, Abby fed Miso out of her hand, bits of fresh tuna, ground beef, eggs, and for a while, he seemed better. Then he stopped eating. She got the vet to show her how to give him IV fluids. The seizures came closer together.

When Abby felt a twinge under her right ribcage, she tried to ignore it. Indigestion, she told herself. Stress.

She stayed up nights, holding the cat, sometimes rocking him like a baby. One night, Eric knelt beside the chair. The cat was still. Abby stroked his fur.

"Sweetheart," Eric said. "Don't you think it's time to let the vet take care of him?"

"By take care of him, you mean put him down."

He nodded. "Yeah."

"You think I'm being selfish. Holding on to him."

"I think there's nothing more you can do. It's time to let him go."

She shook her head. "I feel awful, watching him like this." Her voice wavered. "But I don't want him to die, you know?"

He reached for her hand. "I know you don't. I know."

No more rising moons, no suns. Miso looked for a patch of sunlight but couldn't find it. He wondered where his world had gone. The woman was there and then she was not. He could hear her, and sometimes the man, their voices rustling like birds' wings. In Miso's dream the black dog picked him up by the scruff of his neck and shook and shook him. When the shaking stopped, the woman held him. The taste of salt. The thrum of her heart. Her touch like the lick of his mother's tongue.

Early in the morning, Abby and Eric took Miso in. She held the cat while the vet administered the drug. They discussed cremation, but Abby wanted to bury him in the back yard, so they took him home.

She refused to let Eric help her. "I want to do it myself," she said. In the August heat she stabbed at the garden's hard-baked earth with the shovel. The back door slammed.

Eric came and took the shovel from her. She watched while he dug. She had wrapped Miso in a chenille throw he loved to sleep on. By the time she laid the cat in the hole, his body had gone stiff. So this is what it's like, she thought.

Eric started to fill the hole, but she stopped him. "Let me," she said. She knelt and dragged the dirt over Miso with her bare hands. When it was done, she got up and tamped the dirt down with her shoe.

Eric laid a flagstone over the cat's grave. Arms around each other, they walked back to the house.

The next day, Abby made an appointment with her oncologist. When she saw him a week later, she described the twinge that wouldn't go away.

"How long have you had it?" he asked.

It was hard to look at him. "I don't know. Six weeks, maybe."

He sighed. "Why didn't you call me?"

"The cat was dying."

He examined her breast, the nodes under her arms, her neck, and her groin. He palpated her abdomen. "I don't find anything," he said, "but I want to run some tests. Better safe than sorry."

Abby hated clichés.

The doctor sent her to the lab for blood work and scheduled an MRI for the following Tuesday. She didn't tell Eric. She went alone.

A couple of days after the MRI, the doctor called. She froze when she heard his voice. He never called; his nurse did. "Nothing on the MRI," he said. "I want to see you again in three months. Sooner, if you notice anything that doesn't seem right. Don't put it off, Abby. I mean it. You dodged a bullet this time."

She had been holding her breath. She let it out. "Thank you," she said.

"Don't thank me. Take care of yourself." He hung up.

She sat down at the breakfast room table. Dear God, a reprieve. She wanted to call Eric, but she couldn't. She had kept this scare from him. He would be angry.

She heard barking in the backyard. She looked out. A big black lab was digging at Miso's grave. Abby went out and ran at the dog, yelling, and the dog bolted.

The dog had dug under the flagstone and nudged it aside a little. He'd made only a shallow hole so far, but what if he came back? "It's okay, Miso," she said. "Everything's okay." She filled the hole and moved the stone back into place.

She walked back to the house. She'd left the door open, but it didn't matter. There was no cat to escape, to climb on the porch roof, to bring her dead birds. To demand her lap and pull threads in her sweaters.

"Stop it," she said aloud.

She washed her hands and poured herself a glass of wine. She sat by the window, watching for the dog. They would have to do more to protect Miso's grave. More stones. Maybe a little paved area, a garden with a bench.

After an hour, when there was no sign of the dog, she got up and walked through the house, her steps echoing. In the living room, the piano's presence startled her, as though she'd forgotten it was there. She sat down and touched the keys tentatively. She played scales, limbering her stiff fingers. She didn't expect to remember—it had been months—but the music came: the Debussy preludes and Chopin nocturnes she could never play without crying. Brahms Hungarian dances. Bach preludes and fugues, Beethoven and Mozart and Schubert sonatas.

At times her memory faltered, her fingers stumbled, her hands and arms and neck and shoulders ached. She played anyway, until the house grew dark. She was still playing when Eric came home. He didn't turn on the lights. He stood behind her, kneaded her shoulders, kissed her hair.

APPENDIX

Over her shoes Cynthia wears disposable paper booties that don't conduct electricity. She makes no sound as she moves around the surgical suite, setting up for the next case. It's nearly midnight, and she's been on duty since seven a.m. She was supposed to get off at eleven, after her double shift, but Dan Bowman has sent word he wants her to scrub in on this case, an emergency appendectomy.

Cynthia didn't sleep much the night before. She dreamed that a man, someone she seemed to know but couldn't place, made her lie across the bed facing a mirror while he beat her with his belt. He tried to make her look, but she closed her eyes, and that only made him angrier and more brutal. She woke in a cold sweat, and she hasn't been able to shake the dream all day. It keeps coming back in fragments, especially the image of the man who now seems only vaguely and uneasily familiar. He's stocky like her father, but her father has red hair like hers, and she can't remember her father ever hitting her, even when she was a child. The man in the dream is dark-haired and immaculately dressed. She can't remember his face, only his strength and how his hitting her felt and his yelling at her to watch, damn it. She thinks she's figured out the mirror business. She's thinner than she's been in a long time, but she hates mirrors. She's relieved when she steps out of the shower and the bathroom mirror has fogged over. She avoids her reflection in shop windows. What if the watery image in the glass were to clear, to coalesce, so she sees what she doesn't want to see?

Tonight, the lights in the operating room seem unusually bright. Cynthia's eyes ache. She squeezes them shut. I can do this, she thinks. I can do this blindfolded. The sterile pack lies unopened on the tray, but she knows exactly how she'll place the instruments for Dan, knows how to anticipate his every move during the surgery. They have performed it so often, this seamless, rhythmic dance.

Cynthia opens her eyes as the eleven-to-seven surgical team drifts into the room. Everything is loose and high this time of night. Someone switches on the stereo, and rock music blares. The anesthetist takes his place on the stool at the head of the table and runs a check on his lines and monitors. The phone rings in the holding area, and a minute later, her friend Julia, one of the scrub nurses, comes in. "Okay, folks, look alive! That little girl is on her way up." Cynthia doesn't look at Julia. "Hey, Cynthia! What's eatin' you, girl? You okay?"

Cynthia takes a deep breath. "Sure, Julia. I'm fine. Just tired, that's all."

When Dan Bowman bursts through the double doors, he holds his arms out in front of him, his hands open toward the ceiling. The gesture always reminds Cynthia of some sort of supplication to the gods. She can't read his expression above the mask. He doesn't even look her way. He's gowned and ready. He stands still while Julia snaps on his gloves.

"Evening, all," he says. "Are we ready to relieve this little darling of her nasty appendix? Jody, change that music, will you?"

"Yes, sir, Dr. Bowman. What's your pleasure?"

Dan looks at Cynthia, and an expression crosses his face that makes Cynthia's heart skip. Something is terribly wrong. "How about some country?" he says. "Maybe Emmylou Harris. My wife's coming in to watch me operate. She likes Emmylou."

Cynthia is thankful for the mask. He and Marianna listen to Emmylou? That's Cynthia's music, hers and Dan's. She busies herself with the tray, opens the sterile pack, and places the instruments in order. Cynthia's hands sting inside the gloves. Sometimes the antiseptic soap makes them raw. They distract her now from how hot she feels with Dan's eyes on her. She looks at the wall and blinks away tears. She wants to strip off the gloves and feel how cool the tiles are.

She hasn't seen Dan outside the hospital for over a week. She's tried to reach him on his cell phone, but he hasn't returned her calls. She's called him at home from a pay phone near her house, hoping he'll pick up, but Marianna has answered every time. Cynthia hangs up quickly, seized with the notion that Marianna knows who it is and knows why she calls. Now Marianna is coming here.

Over the last six months, Cynthia and Dan have met whenever he can break away: on his afternoons off, if he can make some excuse to his wife—he has to catch up on charts, or he has a meeting—or late at night when he tells Marianna he's going back to the hospital to make rounds or to do an emergency case. He refuses to go to Cynthia's house. She lives alone in a quiet neighborhood, ten minutes from the hospital. She loves her little house and she wants Dan to like it, too; she wants to show him how she's painted it inside with bright New Orleans colors and filled it with flea market finds and plants and light and music. She fantasizes about an exotic meal, fresh flowers on the table, good wine, candlelight, and going to bed afterward and having him stay all night. All this time now, and he has never been inside it. Her place is too close to the hospital, he says; she knows they have to be careful. She tells herself he's right. When they meet during the day, she parks her car in a mid-town lot and takes a city bus to the stop a block away from the apartment he keeps in an old Italian neighborhood, a good ten miles from the hospital. At night, Dan picks her up at the service station close to her house, or at the Minit-Mart, or at McDonald's; he says it's not safe for her to drive across town late at night.

While they wait for the patient, Dan briefs them on the case. "Ridiculous," he says. "We've got an otherwise healthy fifteen-year-old girl here. I'm pretty sure this kid's appendix has burst. She's been sick as a dog for three days, high fever, tender abdomen, the works, and nobody bothered to bring her in until today. It never ceases to amaze me how people can sit on a situation like this." He looks at the wall clock, turns to Julia. "How much longer, Julia? I'm ready to get this done and get out of here."

"She's on her way up, Dr. Bowman. Should be here any second now."

"Well, it better be soon." Cynthia flinches at his tone.

Cynthia hates Dan's apartment. She knows he shares the expense with two other men, but he won't tell her who they are. Each of them has access to the place at certain predetermined times. There are sometimes traces: the smell of perfume, not hers; a full ashtray; unfamiliar CDs left on the stereo. He tells Cynthia he's worked out every detail so when they're together, it's like they're cut away from the rest of the world. She wants to believe him. She wants to forget the things she heard about Dan when she first went to work at the hospital, but whenever she thinks about how much of his life he spends away from her, she gets a coppery taste in her mouth that seems like fear, like in the dream. She doesn't like to think about how easily he moved into this relationship with her. It seemed as smooth and practiced as his surgical technique, as though he knew by heart the ways to be circumspect, the rules for loving someone other than his wife.

The apartment is comfortable enough, in a spare way. All the rooms are painted the same brilliant white, a finish that shines like porcelain, and the furniture is black with a touch of red or white here and there—red throw pillows on the black couch, black and white photographs hanging in the entrance hall, a red paisley spread on the black lacquered bed. Cynthia thinks the furniture is too modern, angular, and cold. Dan has hung expensive art on the walls, mostly nudes. His favorite painting is an oil of a woman with incredible red hair. The woman's face is obscure, the body segmented like a Picasso nude by slashes of red, abstract and twisted so the only identifiable part is the breast, outlined in black as though a child has traced it with a crayon. Dan says the hair reminds him of her.

His wife's hair is dark, maybe auburn, and short. Cynthia has met her once, at a Christmas party Dan and Marianna gave for the surgery department staff last December. Cynthia didn't want to go, but Dan insisted everybody would notice if she wasn't there. He asked Tom Richards to take her. Tom is a senior surgery resident who knows what's going on between them. He's Dan's

cover in case he can't be reached in an emergency. In
return, Dan sees to it that among the senior residents,
Tom gets good teaching cases. Tom owes him.

The day of the party, Cynthia tried on most of what was in
her closet, but nothing seemed right. She had bought a dress
the winter before in a fit of extravagance, an impractical,
romantic, dark red velvet dress, as iridescent as rubies. She'd
worn it only once, for a candlelight dinner at the apartment
with Dan. He photographed her that night. She drank a
little too much, and she danced barefoot around the
apartment and posed for him. He showed her the black
and white prints a week later. The dress made her look
even thinner, and her hair fell around her face and created
shadows that accentuated her cheekbones and the depth of
her eyes. For one of the shots, he had insisted she lie on the
couch and pose like the red-haired woman in the painting.
Cynthia laughed and asked him if he expected her to contort
that way. But when she saw the photograph, she had to
admit the resemblance was striking. That was his favorite,
Dan said; he promised he would have a print made for her.
He told her she was a work of art.

Cynthia wondered what Dan's reaction would be if
she wore the velvet dress to his party, if it would remind
him of that night. She wanted to excite him in front of
his wife, to taunt him with her presence, since he'd
insisted on it. She put the dress on and stood in front of
the mirror and ran her hands up and down the fabric,
watching its hues change. She unzipped the dress and let
it slide to the floor. She promised herself she would wear
it the next time she and Dan were alone. She decided on
her black silk with the white satin collar. It was beautiful,
tasteful; it seemed like the kind of thing a doctor's wife
might wear.

Cynthia expected Marianna to be tall and unforgivably beautiful, but she wasn't; she was petite and sort of plain. Dan and Marianna were standing in the doorway greeting guests when Cynthia and Tom arrived. Dan stood with one arm around Marianna's waist. She leaned against him.

Dan said, "Marianna, have you met Cynthia Greener? Cynthia's one of the best surgical nurses I've ever worked with. She's my good right arm. Aren't you, Cyn?"

Marianna's eyes didn't waver. "It's so nice to meet you, Cynthia." She took Cynthia's hand in both of hers.

"Marianna, hi. It's nice of you to have us." Cynthia withdrew her hand.

"Dan talks about you all the time," Marianna said. "If you're half as valuable to him as he says, then maybe I ought to be jealous." She looked up at him. "Should I be jealous, Dan?"

"Well, I don't know." Dan grinned at Tom. "What do you think, Tom? Do you think the lady needs to be jealous?"

Cynthia didn't hear what Tom said. She wanted to disappear, to turn and walk into the dark and keep going, but now Dan and Tom were talking about a case they'd done the day before. Cynthia mumbled something to Marianna about how beautiful the Christmas decorations were. Then she gave Dan a dazzling smile, grabbed Tom's arm, and pulled him away.

The rest of the night was a blur, a nightmarish blend of Christmas music and lights and small talk and Dan's attentions to his wife. Marianna was no beauty, but there was an air of confidence about her. Cynthia envied the way she moved, with a fluid grace that made Cynthia feel too tall and clumsy. She wished she had worn the red velvet dress.

~ ~ ~

The doors open and Marianna sweeps in like she's been doing this all her life. She's wearing scrubs, the cap that covers her hair, and paper booties over her shoes. Her perfume fills the room. Cynthia fights the urge to take her own cap off, to free her long red hair, to shake it, to contaminate the room with it. But Dan isn't looking at Cynthia. He's introducing his wife.

"Everybody knows Marianna, I think? Marianna, you remember Jody? And Julia?" Marianna nods, speaks, as he introduces them. Around the table they all mumble something in her direction. "And Cynthia," he says.

The gurney carrying the girl rumbles into the room and the team goes to work. The girl turns and whimpers as they move her from the gurney to the table. Dan talks quietly to her in that way he has. "All right, sugar, you relax. We're gonna take real good care of you, don't you worry."

Near the apartment there's a little hole-in-the-wall Italian restaurant where Cynthia sometimes waits for Dan. She thinks of it as their place and loves it in spite of its shabbiness: blue-and-white checked vinyl tablecloths, cracked plaster walls, chipped, heavy white dinnerware, candles in old wine bottles, years of layers of wax spilling down their sides. She likes its worn-down softness; it's twilight all the time, so unlike the hospital where there's no difference between day and night, where time is always bright and sterile. Most of all, she loves the music Mr. Mattuso, the owner, plays—Italian opera, in honor of his mother, he says. Cynthia has always thought she would hate opera, but the first time she heard Mr. Mattuso's recording of Maria Callas singing Mimi's last aria from

La Boheme, it brought tears to her eyes. Mr. Mattuso sat down at their table and told them the opera's story. He insisted she borrow his CD so she could listen to the entire opera. Dan was impatient that day, sitting there, listening to Mr. Mattuso rattle on. Later, on a cold, rainy Saturday afternoon when Cynthia wanted to get dressed and go out to the record shop around the corner to buy the CD, Dan refused to go with her. He said she was being silly and sentimental. Besides, he said, what if someone saw them? It was a risk he could not, would not, take.

Cynthia takes her place at Dan's right. Marianna walks around to the opposite side of the table and stands back out of the way. While the anesthetist places the mask over the girl's face, Dan keeps talking to her, explaining what will happen, how it will feel to go to sleep. "You'll just drift off, hon. Don't fight it. Before you know it, you'll wake up and it'll all be over, and you'll be out of here in a day or two." The girl is groggy from the pre-op and she fights the mask only briefly. Dan looks at the anesthetist. "Let me know when she's under, Sam." Sam nods. The girl goes completely still, and the anesthetist inserts the breathing tube. For a moment there are just the mechanical sounds of rushing air and beeping monitors playing against a background of Emmylou Harris's melancholy voice. Struck by the girl's pallor and the depth of the dark places under her eyes, Cynthia feels afraid for her. Yet she would trade places with that girl if she could. She would go to sleep and have the hurting thing cut right out of her.

The last afternoon they were together, Dan seemed out of sorts from the beginning. They ate a late lunch at Mattuso's and he found fault with everything about it: the pasta was overcooked, the sauce bland, the music too loud.

When they got to the apartment, he went straight to the refrigerator and took out a beer. He switched on the stereo, switched it off. He stretched out on the couch, picked up the remote control, and started flipping television channels.

Cynthia got a beer for herself and sat on the arm of the couch and stroked his hair. After a few minutes, he sat up and motioned for her to sit beside him. She curled up next to him and they sat like that for a long time without speaking. She was used to his moods; she had learned early on that when he shut himself off, there wasn't much she could do except to wait it out. Eventually, he put his arm around her. "I'm sorry, Cynthia. It's just been one hell of a week."

"Want to talk about it?"

He shrugged. "Nothing out of the ordinary. I was on emergency call at two hospitals over the weekend and I haven't caught up. I can't take it like I used to, I guess." He got up and walked over to the window. "Marianna's on my case, Cyn. I've got to leave here in time to go look at some paint for Michael's room." He was pacing now. "You'd think she could handle that by herself, but she says it's important to Michael for me to go along. She's putting a big guilt trip on me about being away from home so much, you know? And she's watching me like a hawk." He drank the last of his beer and held the empty bottle up to the light, turning the brown glass so the sunlight caught it and threw prisms across the carpet. He stopped and faced her. Cynthia had seen that look on his face only a few times since she'd known him, when he had lost a patient. "Marianna can be very strong-willed."

She chose her words carefully. "Well, if it's important to Michael, you need to go, Dan. She's probably right."

He went back to the couch and held her for a long time. The street noises below sounded very far away to

Cynthia. She remembered what he'd said about this place, that when they're here, they're cut away from the world. That wasn't entirely true. Not anymore.

She went to the bathroom, and by the time she got back, Dan was asleep. His face had gone slack. Not only did he look tired, he looked old. Dan could fall asleep anywhere, any time he could grab a few minutes. It wasn't unusual for him to sleep after they made love, even in the middle of the day. She would stay awake to be sure he didn't oversleep. That day, though, she didn't wake him. She left him a note and slipped out and took a cab back to the parking lot where her car was. The note simply said, "Call me."

The girl lies ready on the table. The anesthetist gives Dan the go-ahead and he makes the incision. The scalpel blade traces a thin line that fills and becomes a dark red mark across the girl's skin. Dan talks as he works, a running narrative about the placement of the incision, the condition of the tissues underneath, the amount of bleeding. All clean, clinical. Marianna steps closer to the table so she's standing directly across from Dan and Cynthia. Cynthia tries to focus on what Dan is doing. She watches his gloved hands, now smeared with the girl's blood. He works quickly, every movement precise, without hesitation. She loves his hands. She thinks they look like a musician's hands, although he swears he's never learned to play an instrument. Cynthia wants him to learn to play the piano.

His voice is cool. "How about a sponge, Cynthia? Little late in the day for daydreaming, don't you think?" He holds his right hand out, palm up.

"Sorry, Dr. Bowman." Cynthia passes him the sponge and checks the count. She makes herself watch as he frees up the appendix, makes herself listen as he explains to

Marianna what he's doing. Marianna leans forward a little, like she's intent on his every move.

Dan looks across the table at his wife. "How you doing, baby? If you start to feel sick or anything, just say so and we'll get you right out of here."

Marianna shakes her head. "I'm fine, Dan. Don't worry about me. I want to see you finish this."

Cynthia wants to turn and look at Dan. She can't remember what color his eyes are—gray, or blue? Marianna's eyes are dark brown above the mask. They shine with reflected light. Cynthia sees the crinkling at the corners of her eyes and wonders, incredulously, if Marianna is smiling. Then she understands why Marianna's here. She knows about Cynthia, and Dan has brought her here to end it.

Cynthia feels sick. The room is suddenly too hot and too cold at once. Dan is still talking; his voice echoes off the tile walls. She fights panic, fights the images of her dream of the beating and the painting with the red slashes like the incision on the girl and the distortion of her reflection in shop windows and the smell of perfume and Marianna's smiling and the sound of Italian arias, all the time going through the motions, watching Dan, anticipating.

"Well, would you look at this?" he says. "She's one lucky kid. I sure as hell thought we'd be in trouble here, but the appendix is intact. No sign of gangrene, either." Dan drops the bloody tissue in the sterile container Julia holds for him and backs away from the table. "Tom, you mind closing? Looks routine. I'm out of here. Come on, Marianna, let's go." He snaps off the gloves as he turns to leave and lobs them into the waste container, then waits for his wife at the doors. "Have a good night, all." The doors open, and Marianna passes in front of him. He follows her and doesn't look back.

The resident has already stepped in and started to close the wound. "Sure, Dr. Bowman. Glad to do your cleaning up for you, any old time. Right, Cynthia?"

Cynthia isn't listening; she's looking at the closed doors. She wants to run after Dan, the hell with Marianna. She wants to stop him and make him explain. She feels suffocated behind the mask, feels her knees give way, but she forces herself to pay attention. Tom's routine is not the same as Dan's. He sutures the wound. It's a nice, clean closure. The girl won't have much of a scar. Dan's right. She is lucky.

Somebody turns off the music. The orderlies move the girl onto the gurney and roll her out, and one by one the surgical team follows. Julia puts a hand on Cynthia's shoulder. "Want to stop for a drink on the way home? Seems like I never see you anymore, Cynthia."

"Thanks, Julia. Not tonight. I'm dead. Next time, though, okay?" Cynthia hopes Julia won't notice her hands are shaking.

"Sure thing." Julia hesitates, then pats her arm. "Take care of yourself." Julia walks out, humming "Gulf Coast Highway." Damn country music, Cynthia thinks. *Damn him.*

Cynthia lingers. She strips off her gloves and the paper cap and booties and tosses them in the waste bin. She doesn't understand why she isn't crying. She should leave, go home, but she can't think of a good reason, even though she works seven to three again tomorrow. She'll have to go soon. The cleaning crew will be in any minute to get this OR ready for the morning. The discarded appendix is still on the tray. Somebody messed up there. It should have gone to the lab. Cynthia opens the container and touches the blob of tissue with one finger. Such a small thing to cause so much pain. So useless to begin with.

CROSSCURRENTS

On the boat to Ship Island, Jana and Eric sat below deck on a wooden bench facing a large woman and four children with carrot-colored frizzy hair and freckled skin like their mother's. The woman wore a loud print dress, its buttons straining over her breasts and stomach. She fanned herself with a folded newspaper. The oldest child, a slight, vacant-looking girl missing her upper front teeth, stared open-mouthed at Jana. Identical twin boys were fighting over a bag of Cheetos. Jana wondered how old the boys were—four, maybe? *With these drugs, multiples are a possibility,* her doctor had said. The youngest, a little girl wearing a faded pink ruffled top and shorts fat with a diaper, clung to the mother and sobbed into her shoulder. When the toddler turned, Jana saw the wide, flat face and almond-shaped eyes of a Down's Syndrome child. Jana shivered. So many things could go wrong.

Eric had said there would be a place to change into her bathing suit on the island, but the thought of dirty stalls smelling of chlorine and sweat and urine had turned Jana's stomach. She'd worn her suit under a pair of shorts and a tank top, and now it wedged into her crotch and bound at the legs and the spandex tummy panel was so tight she could hardly breathe.

The nine o'clock boat on Saturday morning had been sold out, so Eric had booked them for ten-thirty on this one, the smallest and oldest of three boats that crossed the Mississippi Sound to Ship Island and back every day in summer.

"It's the same boat I used to take," he'd said. "It'll be like stepping back in time."

It had rained heavily along the coast the night before and the sky was still overcast. The boat sat dockside, dead still in the murky water, only the occasional slap of a small swell, the water more olive-brown than blue or green, foam on the surface like soap scum. Inside, voices echoed off the metal walls: loud laughter, an older couple sitting behind them arguing, children yelling and crying. It hadn't occurred to Jana that the boat wouldn't be air-conditioned. Sweat trickled down her back. Her thighs stuck to the wooden bench. She thought of cattle cars and slave ships. She glanced at her watch: ten-forty.

"Why aren't we going?" she said.

Eric shrugged. "Beats me."

The little girl across from them had stopped crying. The woman sat her on the floor with a naked baby doll the child slammed against the floor repeatedly. One of the doll's eyes was missing, a black hole.

"You watch her, Lola," the mother said, and the older child slid off the bench and onto her hands and knees. "Boo," she said to the baby. "Boo!" The baby smiled, tears still running down her cheeks, a rivulet of snot on her upper lip. The woman opened her *National Inquirer* and ate a Snickers bar, sucking the melting chocolate off her fingers. The boys found the life vests under the seats and flailed each other with them. The mother said, "Y'all quit that, now!" They stopped but were soon back at it, and from behind her tabloid the mother said, "Boys, if I have to put this paper down, I'm gonna wring your necks." The baby girl toddled the narrow space between their feet toward the center aisle, unsteady on her short legs. When the older sister blocked her way, the baby laughed and did it again until one of the boys stuck out his foot and tripped her.

"Jamie Peets!" the mother said, scooping up the wailing child. "Now look what you done. Shame on you!" She grabbed the boy by the arm and wedged him between her and the window. "Don't you dare move." She turned to the boy on her other side. "You neither, Jimmy."

The boat's engines revved into a loud thrum. The vibration ran though Jana like an electrical current.

"What if I get seasick?" she said.

Eric said, "You won't. The barrier islands keep the water calm."

He had told her about Ship Island. Growing up, he had gone there with his dad and his two brothers, but his parents had divorced when he was fourteen and his mom had moved them back to Ohio, where she was from, and his dad had moved away too and disappeared from their lives. Eric hadn't been back to the Mississippi coast in twenty-five years. Jana had grown up in Atlanta, but she had never been to the Gulf. A convention—Eric was a pharmaceuticals company rep—had meant a trip to Gulfport.

"I can't be this close to the island and not go. Come with me," he had said.

The boat lurched and then eased away from the dock. It rode so low Jana thought if she reached out the window she could trail her hand in the water, like riding in a canoe. The Captain came on the loudspeaker, welcomed everybody aboard, and talked about the weather.

"Already ninety degrees, folks. Gonna be a hot one." He told them to be on the lookout for dolphins, especially on the starboard side. Another crewmember went through the emergency procedures.

Once they were out of the harbor, the boat picked up speed and settled into a steady rhythm. A fine spray misted through the open window, but Jana didn't mind. At least it was cooler. The hormones she had been taking made her hot, nauseated, weepy, and bloated—all the symptoms of early pregnancy without the pregnancy.

The mother rocked and shushed the baby, cutting her eyes at the little boy who looked subdued. "You got a bad, bad brother, don't you, Cissy?"

The baby quieted and tugged at the buttons of her mother's dress. "Titty," she said.

"Oh, Lord. Not right now." The mother rummaged in her big bag and brought out a box of vanilla wafers and gave the child one. The child—Cissy, Jana knew now— threw the cookie on the floor and set up a howl, grabbing at her mother's breasts.

The woman sighed. She unbuttoned her dress and exposed a freckled, stretch-marked, blue-veined breast. The girl made smacking noises while she nursed, kneading her mother's flesh with one hand like a kitten. Jana had never seen breasts that big. The woman made no attempt to cover herself. She looked at Jana. "This botherin' you?"

"No, not at all," Jana said, her face going red. She looked out the window. The sun had come out. Even in sunlight, the water was grayish and dull.

The woman nursed about five minutes on one side, then the other. "There, that's enough," she said, plucked her breast from the child, and buttoned her dress. Milk dribbling down her chin, the little girl climbed off her mother's lap and stood looking up at Jana. She patted Jana's bare leg with one sticky hand.

The mother said, "Would you look at that. She likes you. She don't usually take to strangers."

Jana managed a smile. She found a book in her bag and disappeared behind it, but the baby pounded Jana's legs with both fists.

Jana put the book down. "Hey there," she said to the baby. "Hi, sweetie. Cissy." The baby stretched her arms toward Jana and made little sounds like the cluck of a chicken.

"She wants you to pick her up," the older girl said.

The twin at the window said, "I need to pee."

"Me too," the other boy said.

The mother said to Jana, "I could stand to go myself. You wouldn't mind watching her for a minute, would you?"

Before Jana could think what to say—*Sorry, I can't, I'd rather not*—the woman sat the baby in Jana's lap and used a faded blue washcloth to wipe the child's nose. She offered the cloth to Jana. "I'll leave this with you," she said, "in case Cissy needs it. She's got a little cold."

Speechless, Jana took the dirty rag, stuffed it between her and Eric on the seat, and wiped her hand on her shorts. She hadn't brought any hand sanitizer. The baby felt hot and damp and smelled of urine and something sour. She stood on Jana's lap, her short legs locked straight, and touched Jana's face and hair. The child's eyes were gray, almost translucent, a little bit crossed. Jana's stomach turned.

The mother pointed at the older girl. "Lola's good with Cissy. She knows what to do. Anyway, I'll be right back."

She said to the boys, "Well? Come on." She squeezed between Lola on one side and Eric, Jana, and Cissy on the other. The little boys scrambled after her.

Jana had not noticed the size of the woman's belly while she was sitting. "Eric, did you see that?" she whispered. "I swear I think she's pregnant."

Eric glanced at Cissy. "Surely not. Why would you—"

Jana shook her head. "I can't imagine."

The baby looked around then, her face crumpling, and sat down hard on Jana's lap. "Oh, please don't cry," Jana said. She didn't know what to do with a toddler, let alone one like Cissy. "What does she like, Lola?"

Lola shrugged. "She likes jiggling okay."

Jana bounced her knees. "You mean like this?" Lola nodded. Jana remembered a song from her childhood and sang it.

> *This is the way the ladies ride,*
> *ladies ride, ladies ride,*
> *This is the way the ladies ride*
> *All the way to town, oh.*

Cissy clapped her chubby hands. When Jana stopped, the child nodded vigorously and wriggled.

"She wants to do it again," Lola said.

Another verse, and another. Before long, the baby tired of the game. She rubbed her eyes and nuzzled Jana's breasts, but she didn't cry. Jana rocked her a little, and she fell asleep. Jana explored the idea of her, the weight and warmth against her own body, the wispy red curls, those almond eyes. She wondered how old the mother was; it was hard to tell.

The woman and the twins were gone a long time, it seemed. The little girl grew heavy, and Jana wondered what she would do if the mother didn't come back. But that was crazy; where would the mother go?

There was a commotion behind them. A member of the crew rushed past, carrying a first aid kit.

"Can you see what's going on?" Jana asked Eric.

He stood up, sat back down. "No. Something's happening, though."

Jana shifted the child in her arms and turned to look. A crowd was gathering near the back of the boat. The crewmember shouted, "Everybody in your seats! Give us room!"

Some people did as they were told; others didn't. Jana couldn't see what was happening, either. Then something—a movement, a sound—made her look away from the crowd. A boy and girl, possibly fifteen, sixteen, sat two rows back. The boy's face smooth, almost angelic, no beard, a shock of dark hair over his brow, the girl's bare shoulders tan, her long, blond hair cascading down her back. She was sitting on the boy's lap, touching his face, his hands on her neck and back and in her hair, and they were kissing, deep, searching kisses, oblivious to the ruckus. Jana couldn't bear to watch and yet she couldn't turn away. Since they'd been trying to have a baby, sex with Eric had become all about Jana's hormone levels and cycles, the right day and time, the best chance of conceiving.

It wasn't long before the crowd dispersed. The twin boys came running down the aisle. Their mother yelled at them to stop, but they kept going.

"Sorry it took so long," the woman said, squeezing past Eric's and Jana's legs. "Long line at the restrooms. And somebody fainted back there."

Jana took stock of the big stomach. Yes, she thought, pregnant. The woman took Cissy and sat down next to Lola. Jana's arms felt a little numb and weightless. There was a wet spot on her shorts.

The baby girl stirred and whimpered, then settled. The woman kissed the top of her head.

"Mama missed you," she said, "yes she did." The boys ran past again. "Little hellions. You got kids?" she asked Jana.

"No." Jana stopped herself from explaining although she always felt the need to. She had been married briefly when she was very young, no children. She had sworn she wouldn't marry again, and then Eric had come along six years ago. Eric had never been married. He wanted a child, maybe more than she did. She was thirty-eight years old. They had been trying for a while.

"I got three more," the woman said. "The oldest, Ben? He's eighteen, he just went to the Army." She paused. "I was sixteen when I had him. Jesus, what I didn't know then."

Jana added the numbers. This woman was thirty-four years old, four years younger than Jana. How could that be—a woman like her with seven children, probably another on the way, and Jana couldn't conceive?

"Count yourself lucky," the woman said. "Kids are trouble. Trouble and heartache." She shifted the baby girl and extended her hand to Jana. "I'm Ruby," she said.

Reddened, rough knuckles, dirty nails. Jana didn't want to touch Ruby, but how could she not? She shook Ruby's hand. Warm, moist, the palm callused.

"I'm Jana. This is Eric."

"Hi," Eric said. He stuffed his book in his backpack. "Come on," he said to Jana. "We're almost there. Let's go up on deck."

The island, a long, low slash of white against the dull water of the sound, rose into dunes topped with scrub pines and sea oats. Jana and Eric were among the first off the boat. She looked back for the woman, Ruby, and her children, but she didn't see them. The pier extended far out into the sound, and a long boardwalk led over the dunes to the Gulf beaches. Nearly noon, the sky clear now except for thunderheads lingering far out over the Gulf, the sun directly overhead, the air hot and still, hardly a breeze. The sand burned Jana's feet through her sandals. By the time they reached the top of the dunes, blood rushed in her head and ears and neck, and she was drenched in sweat and out of breath. The horizon tilted dangerously. She stopped, held on to the rail. Her period was six days late. She didn't think Eric had noticed. She hoped he hadn't. She wanted to know for sure before she told him.

Eric said, "You okay?"

She nodded. "God, Eric, is it always this hot?"

"Yeah, in the summer."

To their right, the old fort. To their left, a small concession stand out in the open, no shade. A low, cinderblock building with a sign for restrooms and showers. A small pavilion. In front of them the white sand beach, already crowded with the passengers from the earlier boat, and the water, clear aquamarine out a long way until the color deepened to green, then blue. The surf was higher than Jana had expected.

"You're disappointed, aren't you?" Eric said.

Jana felt sorry for him. He remembered the island through the lens of childhood, the last good days with his father.

"No. It's pretty. The water's beautiful."

Eric suggested they tour the fort first and then spend time on the beach. "I used to find great shells out here," he said. "I don't know about now."

The old fort's brick walls rose thirty feet above the Gulf. Inside, it was cool and damp, a relief from the relentless heat and sun. Eric pointed to the south side. "I used to climb those ramparts." They were standing on the parade ground when Jana spotted Ruby near the foot of a brick tower, the little girl on her hip, Lola beside her.

"Don't you go up there!" Ruby yelled. The twin boys scampered like monkeys up the tower's outside stairs. "Come down right this minute!" she shouted, but the boys hung over the rail around the top, their legs dangling. A guide climbed up and led them back down. He said something to Ruby that Jana couldn't hear. Ruby, whose skin was already turning a hot shade of pink, flushed even deeper. She huffed off, the boys running ahead, Lola trailing behind.

After the fort, Jana and Eric bought hamburgers from the concession stand, a beer for Eric, water for Jana. While she was on the fertility drugs, she couldn't drink. They ate standing up in the pavilion—no seats left—but at least there was shade. They rented chairs and an umbrella and threaded their way among the crowd down to the water's edge and walked east. They passed Ruby and the children. She had spread a blanket near the water line, no chair or umbrella, and she sat with her dress pulled up, revealing her enormous white thighs. Lola seemed absorbed in building a sand castle. The twin boys chased each other in and out of the shallow water, and the baby girl sat in the sand near her mother with a shovel, filling and dumping a plastic pail.

Down the beach, away from the crowd, Eric set up their umbrella and chairs, and Jana took off her tank top and shorts and slathered on sunscreen. She handed the bottle to Eric.

"Do my back?" she said.

Eric rubbed lotion on her back and shoulders. "Hmm. Nice," he said. Her shoulders were tight. He kissed her hair. "There. That good enough?"

She nodded. She wanted to say no, it's not, don't stop, don't ever stop.

Eric moved his chair away from the umbrella. She tossed the sunscreen at him. "Put some on," she said, "or you'll cook."

She sat in the sun for a while, but the sand flies wouldn't leave her alone. "I'm going in the water," she said. "You coming?"

Eric didn't answer. Dozing. Irritated, she walked down to the water. The high surf had carved a ledge in the sand, but then the shore sloped off gradually. She waded in, the cold water a shock after the heat. She was thigh-deep when a wave knocked her down, and then another. She rode the waves and sometimes they took her down and she struggled to get back on her feet. She swam out beyond the breakers and floated on the swells. She felt weightless and small. She thought about the tiny, alive thing that might be swimming inside her, no larger than a seed, its cells doubling and redoubling, all its parts coming together. She had a doctor's appointment the day after they got home. If this treatment cycle failed, she didn't know what they would do. Give up, probably.

She turned from her back and treaded water, looking toward the beach. Eric stood on the shore, waving and calling to her, but she couldn't hear. He waded out, turning sideways against the breakers, and swam to meet her.

After the swim they went for a walk. Tangled ropes of seaweed and piles of broken shells littered the beach. "It must have been stormy out here last night," Eric said. "Heavy surf breaks shells up like that."

Crosscurrents in the surf met in a chaos of spray, the waves played out, and the backwash at the water's edge tugged at their feet. Jana tried to scoop up periwinkles, tiny white, yellow, and purple bivalves, but they burrowed into the wet sand and disappeared, leaving bubbles, then nothing, as though they had never been there at all.

"I picked up a bucket full of these one time and carried them home," Eric said. "Once they're out of water, the shells pop open and the little clams die. They smelled awful. My mother had a fit."

They had walked a quarter of a mile or so when Jana spotted the two kids who'd been making out on the boat. Beyond the breakers and the pale aqua shallows of a sandbar, way out where the water deepened, they splashed and ducked each other and laughed like children.

"Look, Eric." She pointed. "Those kids. They were on the boat with us. Watch them."

The boy and girl came together, treading water, kissing, riding the swells. Jana imagined how they would touch each other under the water, and later, hidden away in the dunes, they would have sex, or maybe not hidden but brazen, right there on the beach, so lost in each other that they didn't care who saw.

"Yeah," Eric said. "I see them." He put his arm around Jana's waist. Their bodies had dried in the sun, their skin salty and hot. He pulled her closer and ran his hand down her back.

"We'll be okay, Jana," he said. "We'll have a baby, and we'll be okay."

They walked on to the end of the island to see the split the hurricanes had made. There were dredges and barges offshore, the work going on to restore the island, but for what, Jana wondered. It would happen again.

They were almost back to where they'd left their stuff when they heard screams. People were running on the beach. Jana and Eric ran, too, toward the sound.

Jana took it all in: Ruby, two park rangers, the faded

blanket, the woman's tote, Cissy's doll and pail and shovel. The twin boys' sunburned shoulders, their round eyes. Lola standing alone at the edge of the water, waves lapping around her feet.

Jana turned in a full circle, scanning the beach and, God, no, the water, for Cissy.

One of the rangers was on a walkie-talkie. "We've got a missing toddler out here. Need assistance." The walkie-talkie crackled.

Jana buried her face against Eric's chest.

"They'll find her," he said. "How far could she get?"

"I need you to describe her, Mrs. Peets," another ranger said. "Hair, eyes. What she's wearing."

"She's two. She's—" Ruby looked at Lola. "Oh Lord, Lola, what's Cissy wearing?"

Lola shrugged.

Jana spoke up. "Pink. Pink top and shorts." Ruby looked at Jana like she'd never laid eyes on her.

The ranger wrote it down.

"Redheaded, like me," Ruby said. "Gray eyes, like her daddy's." Ruby fluttered her hands around her face like she was batting away flies. "She's got the Down's. Not too bad, see, she's a smart girl. She wouldn't run off."

The rangers looked at each other. One said, "Where'd you last see her?"

Ruby pointed at the blanket, her hand shaking. "Right here," she said. "She was right here a little bit ago."

The other ranger knelt beside Lola and brushed the child's hair out of her eyes.

"Hi, sweetheart," he said. "Don't be scared. Did you see where your little sister went?"

Lola shook her head.

The ranger said, "It's all right if you don't know. But you can tell me if you do."

She looked at Ruby, then toward the water. "I told Cissy not to," she said, "but she don't mind me." Lola's thumb went in her mouth.

Ruby's voice rose to a keening. "Oh," she said, "oh Lord. Oh Jesus." She sank heavily to the blanket. One of the twins, then the other, sat beside her and patted her arms. Lola dug in the wet sand with her bare hands.

Jana and Eric waited in line to board the boat back to Gulfport, the cacophony of the beach replaced by stunned murmuring among the crowd, the crackle of walkie-talkies, the rangers' voices over bullhorns, organizing the search of the dunes. A Coast Guard rescue boat trolled offshore. Ruby sat in the shade of the pavilion with the other three children who were eating popsicles. A woman park ranger sat with them. How long would Ruby have to wait?

"Did you hear?" a woman behind Jana said. "That woman fell asleep and left the older girl to watch the baby and those rowdy boys. What kind of mother does that? All those people around, and lifeguards. Why didn't somebody see her? Poor little thing."

Jana faced the woman. "That little girl has a name," Jana said. "Her name is Cissy."

Near the front of the line, the teenage couple stood a little apart, the sunburned girl looking back toward the beach, arms crossed over her breasts. The boy slouched against the boardwalk rail. He tucked the girl's damp hair behind her ear, but she didn't seem to notice.

As the boat left the island dock, a thunderstorm blew in and stirred up the waters of the sound. Jana rested her head on Eric's shoulder. She looked out the window and remembered Cissy's odd face and eyes, her short legs, how she'd clapped her hands and touched Jana's face and hair. She imagined a calm place deep in the waters of the Gulf where light played like stars on the surface and the currents flowed gently and the wind and lightning couldn't reach, the baby floating there, turning somersaults and cartwheels, swimming, her eyes open to the wonder.

SPARROW, SPARROW

Sunday mornings when Mama sleeps late, my older sister, Charlene, and I clamber over her in the bed like pups nuzzling for a teat. Mama wakes and swats at us and says, Leave me alone, but she gives in and takes our shivering, scrawny little selves under her covers. Our daddies have moved on by then. We don't have the same one. The other men have not started coming around yet. It's just Mama, Charlene, and me. We are enough.

Later, men come and go. They are not even our stepdaddies. The summer I'm eleven and Charlene is fourteen, there's a man who sticks around a while, until Mama catches him with his hands on my sister. Mama swears off men after that. She takes to her bed and reads the Bible and weeps. Her lamentation, she says, for her sins. We girls are marked by her sin, she says. I, Lura, was born with dark marks on both sides of my neck like fingerprints as though, Mama says, the devil had hold of me and didn't want to let me be born. She says Charlene's mark is her beauty.

By the time Charlene is sixteen, she wants to drop out of school and get a job. Any job would be better than that hellhole, Charlene says, but Mama says, Watch your mouth in front of your sister, and No, you've got to finish. I don't want you girls turning out like me.

I want whatever Charlene wants. I am her shadow. She tells me to go away, but I don't. At night I like to watch her brush her hair before bed. I'm awake when she gets up and goes to the window and stands there, naked, looking out. I wonder what she sees, or if she sees anything at all. I get up and wrap a blanket around her. Go back to bed, I say. Go to sleep.

At dinner on the grounds after church, Charlene shuns the boys and stands off to the side in the shade. She sucks her thumb the way she used to when she was little and dances in one spot, like she hears music nobody else can hear. Her hair, pale, glossy gold and curly, falls about her shoulders and moves with the breeze. That hair alone is a beacon of temptation, Mama says. At home Charlene goes around singing little songs she makes up in her head. Charlene's songs are not like music you hear on the radio or TV. Whatever her eye falls upon becomes a song in that moment and then it's gone. I ask her why she won't write them down and she says they aren't meant for anybody else to hear. Until she meets a man named Otha Sparks who plays guitar in a band.

Where'd you meet him? Mama asks.

Somewhere, is Charlene's answer.

The first time Otha comes to the house, his dark hair is tied back in a ponytail. His skin looks weathered like he works outdoors, the tips of his fingers are callused from playing. He seems a lot older than Charlene. He wears earrings. A tattoo shows below his rolled-up shirtsleeve. The part I can see looks like feathers, and I yearn to see the rest. He follows Charlene around with a little black machine and records her songs.

The second time he comes, he brings his guitar. Mama has washed her hair and put on a pretty dress and her favorite boots made of real, finely tooled leather. She cooks dinner, but she and I are the only ones who eat. Charlene and Otha snuggle on the couch, her back to him, his arms cradling her and the guitar, his left hand over hers on the frets, moving her fingers to make chords, their right hands joined, strumming. Mama watches like a guard dog. I close my eyes and sway to the music, moving my lips, forming words without sound. I cannot carry a tune.

Otha books Charlene at a bar in Memphis. A gig, he calls it. It's small, he says, but it's a start. Charlene practices on the guitar, but her rhythm is wrong. Even I can tell that.

Otha says, Don't play. Sing. I'll do the rest. He strums along as her songs come for the first and only time. He scribbles in a notebook, and the recorder is always, always on.

Otha tells Mama he needs to take Charlene to some clubs. If she's gonna sing in a place like that, she's got to see what it's like, he says. She don't need to get up there before a crowd the first time without ever having set foot in a club.

She's under age, Mama says.

Otha puts his arm around Mama and says, Don't you worry. I'll take care of her.

He and Charlene go out a lot and stay out late. I try to wait up till she comes in, but sometimes I can't. I wake, though, when she slips in her bed. I hear her singing softly.

~ ~ ~

Otha buys Charlene a red dress, shiny with sequins. It skims her body like light.

Mama says, Wait. She goes to her room and comes back with the boots. Try these on, she says to Charlene.

The boots fit. Charlene flits about the room and preens like a red bird, poised to fly.

The afternoon Otha comes to pick Charlene up to take her to Memphis, she's not wearing the pretty dress and the boots. She refuses to come out of our room. Otha stands outside the door.

Come on out now, Otha says.

She says, I can't go, Otha.

Stage fright, he says. It's natural, your first time.

Finally, she opens the door.

Get dressed, Otha says, and she does. She comes out looking pale and trembly, her mascara smeared from crying, her eyes glassy with fear.

He practically carries her to the car. As they drive away, I blink at the bright sunlight reflected off Otha's rear window. I can't see my sister for the glare, but I imagine her face pressed to the glass, looking back towards home.

Mama and I wait up. By midnight Mama is pacing. I never should have let her go, she says. Otha brings Charlene home at two in the morning. Charlene's eyes are red and swollen. She storms off to our bedroom and slams the door.

Mama stands with her hands on her hips. She says, What'd you do to her, Otha?

He says, Don't look at me, I didn't do nothing. When it came time for Charlene to sing, she wouldn't go up on the stage. She said she didn't have a song in her head.

~ ~ ~

At home, though, Charlene sings. Her songs have always been quiet little things, almost whispered, but now she bursts out singing. Mama says it's like some people speak in tongues.

One night Otha brings a computer to the house. He sits down and we gather round while he puts in a CD. Out comes Charlene's voice, only it doesn't sound like her.

Audio-engineered, Otha says.

Charlene gets up and leaves the room.

Otha gets Charlene another gig, this time at a roadhouse across the state line in Alabama. She'll do fine, he says. That first time was just the jitters.

But when he brings her home, she's not wearing her shiny dress and Mama's boots, and Otha has tight lines around his mouth. It happened again, he says. She couldn't sing. Or she wouldn't.

He gets in his car and speeds away. We don't know it then, but we won't see him again.

It's September. Charlene refuses to go to school. I have to go and Mama is working, so Charlene is home alone. I ask Mama if she's worried about her and she says no.

If I had a dollar for every man who's left me, Mama says, I'd be rich.

I get home from school one afternoon and Charlene is gone. She doesn't come home that night or the next. When she shows up on the third day, I think Mama must be too scared by how sick Charlene looks to yell at her because Mama puts her to bed. That night, Charlene moans in her sleep. I'm scared, but eventually, I fall asleep, too. Sometime in the dark hours of morning, Charlene calls out, Mama? Mama? Mama comes in and snaps on the overhead light. Charlene is standing there with blood streaming down her legs.

What have you done, Mama says, Oh sweet Jesus, Charlene. What have you done?

Charlene spends a few days in the hospital and I'm afraid she'll die, but she doesn't. When she comes home, she hardly speaks. There are no songs. The house without her voice might as well be a tomb. After a couple of weeks Mama arranges with the school for Charlene to catch up on the work she's missed and makes her go. Kids whisper and snicker behind Charlene's back, but she doesn't seem to notice. She moves through the world like she's the only one in it. At night in our room she gets in her bed and turns her face to the wall. I crawl in beside her and tell her everything will be all right, but she pushes me away.

You don't know, she says. You don't know.

I guess I don't, I say.

But I want to.

One morning I wake and Charlene's not in her bed. Mama sits at the kitchen table, crying. Mama's suitcase and some of Charlene's clothes are gone. Mama's boots are gone too but the sequined dress hangs in the closet.

I think I know where Charlene might go. Someplace quiet, where her songs will come back to her. When I tell Mama I believe I could find Charlene, she touches the mark on the side of my neck.

No, she says and folds me in her arms. Rocks me a little. Holds on. And then she's singing, her mouth right against my ear, and I know it's one of Charlene's little breathless songs. Mama's voice is clear and soft, like hers.

Little sparrow with one bruised wing,
Sweet bird, who taught you how to sing?
Who made you fall
And stopped your song
And never picked you up at all?
Rise up on your unbroken wing
And sing, sweet sparrow, sparrow sing.

I push Mama away. I'm crying. How do you know her song?

I wrote it down, Mama says. She pulls me in, cradles my head against her breast. I can feel the beating of her heart. She sings the song again, and this time, I join in, my flat voice a whisper.

THE ONE TO GO

Paula went to the door on a Friday afternoon, expecting the UPS man, and there stood a scrawny teenage girl with bleached, shaggy hair, multiple piercings, and a tight tee shirt riding up over her pregnant belly. A handsome African-American kid with long dreadlocks hovered behind her. It took Paula a second to realize that the girl might be her husband Barry's daughter. This girl bore little resemblance to the photographs that lined their front hall.

"Mallory?" Paula said.

The girl shoved her hands in her jeans pockets. "Yes. Who are you?"

"I'm Paula. I'm your dad's wife." Paula's hand went to her heart. "Oh my god! Come in, come in." She held the door open for Mallory and the boy. "Wait here. I'll get your dad." Barry was in his study, grading papers. Paula hurried down the hall, past the wall of photographs. "Barry! Mallory's here. She's home!"

"What?" Barry came out of his study and stopped, mouth open, like he'd been punched. "Mallory?" He covered the length of the hall in a few strides and took

Mallory in his arms. He held her a long time. The boy stood with his arms crossed, looking on.

Mallory wriggled out of his arms. "Hi, Dad," she said.

Paula blinked away tears. "Let's go in here," she said, motioning to the den. "Can I get you something? Have you eaten?"

"Karim might like a beer," Mallory said.

"We don't have any," Paula said. "We have Cokes. That's all."

"A Coke will do," Mallory said. She patted her stomach. "I can't have a beer anyway."

Barry and Mallory led the way, not touching now. Paula and the young man followed. Paula got Cokes for everybody. They sat in the den. Karim was the baby's daddy. He was twenty-two. He worked on an offshore oilrig, three weeks on the job and one off. All this in a rush from Mallory. They were living together in an apartment on Foley Street, west of downtown. Paula knew that neighborhood, and so did Barry: run-down houses and old apartment complexes, razor wire on the fences, iron bars on windows. Not a good place to live. Paula was surprised when Barry didn't react. Maybe he was too stunned.

Paula was stunned, too.

She had never met Mallory. The girl had run away when she was thirteen, two years before Paula and Barry married. Barry had still borne the scars when Paula met him: dealing with private detectives, hounding the police to no avail, placing ads in cities like San Francisco, Los Angeles, Chicago, New York, Denver, Portland. All the dream places kids ran to. Paula had believed that Mallory must be dead, but she'd never said so to Barry. Now here Mallory was.

Barry took off his glasses and wiped his eyes. "Where have you been all this time?"

"Here and there," Mallory said. "California for a while. That's where I met Karim." A gap of skin showed between Mallory's tee shirt and her low-riding jeans. A tattoo snaked down her hip and disappeared.

Barry said, "You could have let us know you were all right. Do you have any idea what it was like for me— searching and searching and not finding you?"

Mallory chewed a fingernail, polished black. "I guess."

"You guess what?"

"I guess I might have called."

Barry struggled to light his pipe. His reaction to Mallory shocked Paula. She would have thought he would welcome the girl, no questions asked. Instead, he seemed angry. He was grilling her. He had been a wreck when Paula first knew him—harried, distracted, always a five o-clock shadow and deep circles under his dark eyes.

He took his time and drew long on the pipe before he spoke, watched the spiral of smoke. Mallory and Karim looked at each other. Paula knew it was a strategy, something Barry did when he was collecting himself, holding back. "Why did you decide to come home? Why now?"

"We wanted to settle somewhere. Because of the baby. We're not here because we need, like, money or anything."

"Are you married?"

"No," Mallory said. "Marriage is nothing but a piece of paper, Dad. Look what marriage did for you."

"The marriage to your mother wasn't all bad, Mallory. It gave me you." He turned to the young man. "Karim. That's an interesting name."

"My mother liked it," Karim said. He touched the back of Mallory's neck, her hair.

"Are you Muslim?" Barry gestured with his pipe. "Not that it matters." Barry was the most liberal person Paula knew, but his face was flushed, the muscle in his jaw worked. Maybe he wasn't so liberal when it came to his own daughter.

"What if I am?"

Paula shot Barry a look, shook her head. She said, "When's the baby due, Mallory?"

"February."

"Do you know what it is?"

"No." So no prenatal care, probably. They would have to get her to a doctor.

Karim stood and took Mallory's hand. "Come on. Let's go."

Mallory got up off the couch and stretched her back. She was too thin except for her rounding belly.

Barry hugged her again. "I'm so glad you're home."

Mallory backed away. "I'm not *home*. I'm not your little girl anymore."

"Well," Barry said, glancing at her stomach. "That's true. I'm glad you're *back*."

Mallory shrugged. "See you guys later," she said.

"Call us," Paula said. She opened her arms to hug Mallory, but the girl walked past her. Too soon, Paula thought. She would have to take it slow.

Paula and Barry watched the old Toyota pickup pull away. "Are you okay?" she said.

"I don't know." His voice broke. "It's like she's come back from the dead. But seeing her like this. Pregnant, by that kid? My God."

"But she's here," Paula said.

Barry ran his hands through his thinning hair. "It's unbelievable. I'm thankful. Really, I am." He looked at Paula. "But what are we going to do?"

Paula couldn't answer him. She didn't know what to do, either. She hadn't bargained for Mallory. The girl's presence would change everything.

~ ~ ~

They didn't hear from Mallory for a couple of weeks. When she finally called, she told Paula that everything was great. Karim was away, working.

"Have you seen a doctor? An obstetrician?" Paula asked.

"No! I know girls who had babies on the street, and they did okay."

Paula cringed. "But you're not on the street. You're here. It's important to take care of yourself and the baby. I'll go with you, if you want me to."

"Oh, all right." Paula could almost hear Mallory's shrug over the phone.

The day of the appointment, Paula picked Mallory up. Paula hated the women's clinic, those awful little exam rooms. The instruments on the counter, the table with its paper covering, and the stirrups were enough to make her break out in a sweat.

Mallory was a little anemic, the doctor said. The baby was small for its gestational age. He gave Mallory prenatal vitamins, another appointment, and a schedule of free childbirth and labor classes at the state health department.

"That wasn't so bad, now was it?" Paula said, her own heart racing, her hands cold. Mallory slumped against the passenger door. She looked more scared than angry, and Paula wanted to touch her. "Everything's going to be all right, Mallory," she said. When she pulled up in front of the apartment complex, Mallory got out without a word and walked away. No thank you, no goodbye.

Paula leaned her head against the steering wheel. She didn't know how to be a mother. She didn't even know what Barry expected of her. For his sake, she supposed, she had to try. That night, she suggested that they invite Mallory and Karim for supper.

"Good idea," Barry said.

The night that Mallory and Karim came, Paula made vegetarian chili and corn bread. Mallory wore the same tee shirt she'd worn that first day, but her belly had grown. Paula made a mental note to offer to take her shopping.

Over dinner, Barry said, "Tell us about yourself, Karim."

Karim kept right on eating. "There isn't much to tell."

"Yes, there is," Mallory said. "Karim went to UCLA. He was going to be a film major."

"Really?" Barry said. "You dropped out? How'd you end up working the rigs?"

Karim was on his third beer. He tapped the nearly empty bottle on the table. "It's good money. I got tired of school."

"Well," Barry said. "It's honest work. Somebody's got to do it."

"Dad. Don't talk down to Karim."

Paula scraped her chair back. "Can I get anybody anything? More chili, Karim?"

"I'm not talking down to him. I'm curious. Where'd you grow up?"

"LA projects. Just what you'd expect, Mr. Kimbrell."

"I don't *expect* anything," Barry said.

"Mallory, tell your dad about the doctor visit," Paula said.

Mallory rolled her eyes. "What about it?"

"The due date? Hearing the baby's heartbeat?" She said to Barry, "The nurse let me listen. That was amazing."

"Dad isn't interested in all that."

Barry leaned his elbows on the table. "I'm interested. That's my grandchild."

Mallory's voice faltered. "The baby's fine. We're all fine. Aren't we, Karim?"

"Sure, Mal," he said. She rested her head on Karim's shoulder. Her shirt rode up a little more, revealing a bruise, already fading to yellow, on her side. Paula went cold when she saw it. She looked away, then back at Mallory. She had pulled her shirt down.

Had Paula imagined it? She got up. "How about some apple pie and ice cream?"

"I'll help," Barry said. They left Mallory and Karim sitting at the table. When they went back to the dining room, they were gone.

"Well," Paula said. "So much for that." They cleared the table. Should she tell Barry what she'd seen? There could be a hundred reasons for a bruise.

Paula answered Karim's call the day the baby came. "We had a boy. Six pounds, seven ounces. They're both okay." There was no need for Paula and Barry to come to the hospital. They had named the baby Ali.

When the baby was a week old, Paula and Barry carried a meal to the apartment—pot roast and vegetables, rolls, and a lemon pie. They went uninvited, which made Paula nervous, but surely Mallory needed some help. Mallory invited them in—Karim wasn't there—and they took turns holding the baby. Paula was forty-eight years old and had never held a newborn. With his knees drawn up, Ali fit the length of her forearm. He had a nicely shaped head, a shock of black hair, and mocha-colored skin like Karim's. He fell asleep in Paula's arms. His mouth twitched at the corners, almost a smile. Paula was overcome with longing for what she had missed.

On the way home, Paula and Barry talked about the state of the apartment: a mattress on the floor, an old-fashioned dinette table and two folding chairs, a futon, dirty diapers everywhere, beer cans scattered about.

"At least there were the lights," Paula said.

"What lights?"

"You didn't notice? They have little lights, like Christmas tree lights, strung all around the rooms. That's kind of sweet, don't you think?"

"It's a sty," Barry said. "And my daughter and grandson are living in it."

"They need a crib," Paula said.

"Buy one, then," he said. The next day, she ordered a baby bed and had it delivered.

Paula and Barry argued over what to do next. "She's seventeen years old," Paula said. "She needs help, especially if Karim's working off shore. I think we shouldn't wait for her to call. I think we should go over there, like we did when we took the meal."

"I don't think she wants us, Paula."

"Maybe it's me she doesn't want." Paula teared up. "Think about it. She went away, and you married me. Before, there was just the two of you. It's like I took her place. Maybe she resents me."

Barry said, "She didn't leave you. You had nothing to do with it."

"I can't believe we're arguing over this," Paula said. But she could believe it. Mallory's return was taking its toll—on her, on Barry, on the marriage.

Early on a Thursday morning, Mallory called and asked them to babysit that afternoon. "It's a good sign, don't you think?" Barry said. "But I have a committee meeting late afternoon, after my last class."

Paula didn't have any classes on Thursday afternoons. "I can keep the baby," she said.

"You don't mind?"

"Not at all." She remembered how it had felt to hold Ali. "I'll enjoy it."

She didn't enjoy it, though. When Barry got home at five-thirty, she was pacing with the screaming child. "Mallory didn't leave enough milk," she said over Ali's wailing.

Mallory didn't show up until nine.

"Where were you?" Barry said, handing over the baby.

Mallory sat on the couch, lifted her shirt, and unhooked her nursing bra, exposing a breast. Paula wished she would cover herself. Barry looked away.

"I interviewed for a job, Dad."

"A job? Until nine o'clock?"

"Well, no. Karim and I got a burger, and then we went to a movie."

Paula said, "I tried to call you, Mallory. You shouldn't turn your phone off when we have the baby. What if we—"

Mallory took away her breast. "If you don't want to keep Ali, say so. I'll get somebody else." The baby screwed up his face and started to howl. Mallory pulled down her shirt without bothering to fasten the bra. The shirt clung to her nipple, a wet circle of milk spreading.

"It's not that we don't want him," Paula said. "We were worried. We ran out of milk."

"Sorry. I won't bother you anymore."

Mallory wrapped the crying baby in a sling, stuffed things in the diaper bag, and slammed the door on her way out.

A few days after the babysitting fiasco, Paula noticed a peculiar smell in the den, a little like condensed milk—

sweet, but soured. Breast milk, Paula thought; that's it. She had fed the baby there. She'd missed something when she cleaned up—a burp cloth, a piece of his clothing.

Barry was dozing on the couch. "Barry?" She nudged him. "Move. I need to look under the cushions."

He stumbled up. "What's the matter?"

"Don't you smell it?"

He blinked, sniffed. "I don't smell anything."

She pulled the cushions off and looked for stains. She dug in the crevices. She got down on her hands and knees and checked under the couch.

"If you'd tell me what you're looking for, maybe I could help."

Barry would think she was crazy. "Never mind." She put the cushions back. "Sorry I woke you."

The sour smell lingered in the house like a reminder. On Saturday, Paula suggested they buy some things for Ali and take them to the apartment. "It's a gesture. We can let her know we're not angry."

"I'm not angry," Barry said. He put down the book he was reading. "No, that's not true. I'm angry as hell. Every time I think about her with Karim—"

"If she could survive on the street in California, I think she'll be all right."

Barry stared at her. "You don't get it, do you? You never had a child. You can't imagine what it's like to have Mallory turn out this way."

Paula grabbed her purse and keys. "You're right. I don't know what that's like. But I'm learning."

She left the house and drove around for a while. Barry was only partly right. During graduate school, Paula had lived with a boy named Tony who was a lot like Karim— exotic, a little dangerous. Tony was into drugs, but she loved him—or she thought she did. One night, he came in stoned and hit her. The next morning, he cried and swore he'd never do it again. For a while, he didn't. But when he did, she needed stitches. A few weeks later, she realized she was pregnant. She was working towards a PhD in women's studies. A baby would ruin everything. She moved out and took care of it herself. She had never told anybody about that baby, not even Barry. Sometimes she imagined the child she'd gotten rid of. It would have had dark hair, like Ali. It would have been beautiful and very, very smart.

She wound up at Target, buying diapers and a couple of onesies, a teething toy, a board book version of *Goodnight, Moon*. Driving through the neighborhood where Mallory lived, Paula locked her doors. At the apartment, she could hear the TV going, but nobody came to the door when she knocked. She wedged the bags up against the doorframe and hoped nobody would steal them. She went to the park and walked the track to clear her mind.

When she got home, Barry had left a note: Jogging, be back in an hour. He was jogging a lot these days, almost obsessively. She wondered sometimes what he was running away from. He had written the time, two-thirty, and signed it with X's. Making up to her. It was after five, and his car was gone. He had come home and left again.

She called his cell phone and got his voicemail. "Call me," she said.

She had a set of introductory-level women's studies "Who Am I?" personal essays to grade by Monday. She read a few, but they set her teeth on edge. Most of the young women she taught seemed naïve and idealistic. Some of them were little feminist firebrands, ready to take on the world. Life would take care of all that, she

supposed. She made tea and sat on the deck and drank it.
She closed her eyes and tried to relax, but anxiety nagged
at her. Where was Barry? She tried his cell phone again.
This time, he answered.

"Sorry," he said. "I should have called."

"Where are you? I was worried."

"I've got Mallory and the baby. We're on our way
home."

"Barry? What—" He hung up.

He was bringing them *home?* Without asking her.
Paula wasn't sure there was room in that house for her
and for Mallory, too. She forgot about the grading. She
paced. Half an hour later, she heard Barry's car. She turned
on the carport light and walked outside. Mallory got out
of the car and walked past Paula into the house without
speaking. Barry got the crying baby out of the car seat.
Barry looked ashen and angry.

"What happened?" Paula said.

"Let's get her settled. I'll tell you later." Barry put his
arm around Paula. "You don't mind that I brought her
home, do you?"

Mallory was Barry's child. His resurrected child. Paula
said, "No. I don't mind."

Mallory went straight to her old room and closed the
door. Paula heard her crying, imagined her crying in that
room before she ran away from home, plotting her escape
from whatever had troubled her. A child, on her own like
that. There was something admirable about it.
Courageous. Strong. Paula had been strong, too, in her
own way.

Barry went out for diapers and formula to supplement
the night feedings. Paula set up the portable crib in their
bedroom and moved the rocking chair there. She gave
the baby a bottle of breast milk. Ali took the bottle and

seemed to want more. "Poor little guy," she said. She rocked him even after he slept. Several scenarios ran through her mind, none of them good. She put the baby in the crib and slipped out.

Barry was sitting in the dark den. She turned on a lamp and sat beside him. "So tell me."

He sighed. "Mallory called me while I was out jogging. Karim was due home Saturday. When he didn't come, she said she didn't think much about it. Sometimes he works weekends because the pay is good. She kept trying his cell, no answer. This morning, she called the rig's onshore office. They told her Karim left last Saturday, on schedule. I wanted to call the police and report him missing, and that's when she went to pieces. She wouldn't say, but I figure it means he's been in some kind of trouble. She says he's done this before, and he's always shown back up. He took the truck, so she's been stuck in that apartment."

"Oh, my god," Paula said. She went to the bar and poured each of them a Scotch. Barry swirled the liquor in the glass. He reached for her hand. They sat for a long time, not talking.

Bill collectors came to Barry and Paula's house, looking for Karim. He owed rent. He owed utility bills. He owed a payday loan company. Mallory got a text message from Karim. He was working in Texas. She wept and flounced around dramatically, but she stayed. She left wet towels on the floor. She put soiled diapers in whatever trashcan was handy. She came to the table, ate, and either watched TV or went back to bed. Paula cleaned up after Mallory, did the laundry, prepared meals. If she weren't so exhausted, she could almost laugh at the irony: the women's studies professor reduced to a cliché, chief cook and, literally, bottle washer.

The smell of breast milk permeated everything, the upholstery, Paula's clothes, the air. She wasn't imagining it. She found used nursing pads everywhere: on the end tables in the den, between the sofa cushions, tossed on the floor. Paula showed them to Mallory before she put them in the garbage can.

"Please throw these away," she said. "They smell."

"No, they don't," Mallory said.

"You're used to it. We're not."

Was this Paula's punishment? She lay awake nights, imagining a fetus the size of the tip of her little finger.

One afternoon, Paula got home early. Barry had come by her office and told her he was leaving campus too, to go jogging. "I won't be long," he'd said.

The house was quiet. Paula thought Mallory and the baby were napping until she heard Mallory's voice coming from the den. When she walked in, Mallory said, "Got to go" and shut off her phone.

"Was that Karim?" Paula said.

"What if it was?"

"Is he back?" From the look on Mallory's face, Paula knew he was. "Oh, Mallory. Don't do this."

"He says he's sorry about leaving us. He wants us to come back to the apartment. Everything's going to be okay now."

Paula sat down across from her. "Mallory, honey, I need to tell you something. I saw the bruise on your side the night you and Karim came here for dinner." Mallory started to get up, but Paula held her arm. "Wait. Hear me out. If you go back to him, he'll hurt you. Believe me. I know."

Mallory pulled away. "You don't know me. You don't know Karim, either."

Paula got up. "You're right. I don't."

She tried to call Barry and got no answer, not even his voice mail. It was just as well. Let him talk to Mallory. Let him deal with her. It was time to start supper. She went to the kitchen. Maybe a risotto. Something about the mindless stirring always calmed her.

When the doorbell rang, Paula's first thought was Karim. Had Mallory told him to come over? How would she handle it—not answer the door? Call Barry? Call the police? The bell rang again. She looked through the peephole and saw two policemen. My god, she thought, what now?

Paula and Mallory sat apart on the couch, Ali in Paula's lap. The policemen sat opposite them. Barry had been hit by a car. He died at the scene.

On the side table, Barry's reading glasses, a stack of papers, books he hadn't gotten around to. His jacket thrown over a chair. Paula picked up the jacket and held it to her face.

One of the policemen asked if he could call someone. Paula said she would do it.

She didn't call anybody that night. How would she say it? *Barry had an accident. Barry was killed. Barry was the victim of a hit and run. Barry was gone. Barry was dead.*

Around nine o'clock, she couldn't stand Mallory's hysterics any longer. "Go to your room," she said, like she might order a ten-year-old. "Take Ali with you."

"But—"

"For god's sake, Mallory. Go."

Paula lay on Barry's side of the bed. She imagined the car careening into him, saw him lying on the pavement. She was awake at three in the morning when Mallory came to her door. She looked so small, standing there, silhouetted by the hall light.

"Can we stay with you?" Mallory asked. "Please?"

"All right," Paula said. Mallory got into bed and laid Ali between them. After Mallory slept, Paula cuddled the baby. She listened to the snuffling sounds Ali made in his sleep. How simple it seemed, that breathing in and out.

Early the next morning, the phone started ringing. Neighbors and colleagues from the college came to the house. Barry's best friend offered to go with Paula to identify Barry and make the arrangements.

She hadn't thought about a funeral. "I don't know what he wanted," she said. "We never talked about it."

Mallory was sitting in Barry's favorite chair, her legs drawn up under her. Her eyes were red from crying. "Dad used to say he wanted a party. I was eleven when his mother died. He hated her funeral. After it was over, he said he didn't want a funeral. Nonsense, he called it. 'If you want to do something, throw a party. Food, wine, the works.' That's what he said."

"You're serious," Paula said. Mallory nodded.

Paula spent the afternoon doing what had to be done. That night, she and Mallory sat at the kitchen table. There was a lot of food, but neither of them ate. Paula moved Barry's chair away from the table. She couldn't stand to look at it. Paula was on her second Scotch.

Mallory said, "My mother. Should we let her know?"

Barry had told Paula the story about his ex-wife the first time Paula went to dinner at his house. He'd shown her the photos in the hall of Mallory from the time she was an angelic newborn until she was a sullen thirteen-year-old. There, the photos stopped. There were no photos of Mallory with her mother. Barry and his ex-wife, Janice, had divorced when the child was three. Barry got full custody because Janice didn't want her. Janice moved away and had no contact with them for a couple of years. Barry came home from the college one day, and Janice was there, sitting on the floor, playing with Mallory. The sitter had let her in. Janice had changed her mind. She wanted her child, after all. She stayed long enough for Mallory to start to trust her. When she left again, Barry said, the second betrayal was far worse than the first. Mallory, a sweet, compliant child, began to have night terrors and tantrums. Later, she got into fights in school, dabbled in drugs, and lashed out at Barry in awful, stormy scenes—a downward spiral that had culminated in her running away.

Paula had no knowledge of what Mallory's mother was like except what Barry had told her. She sensed that Janice wasn't cut out to be a mother, either. The last person Paula wanted to see at Barry's funeral was Janice, but she said, "It's up to you. Whatever you want to do is fine with me."

The baby sucked hungrily at Mallory's breast. "I don't want her here. Dad wouldn't, either."

Barry was cremated. There was a brief service in the campus chapel the following Friday. After, friends gathered at the house. They ate and drank and told good stories about Barry. How could Paula not have known that a party was what he wanted? Were there other things she didn't know? There must be. She'd kept her own secrets, things she'd never told Barry. That she was wild like Mallory when she was young. That she'd gotten rid of the only child she would ever have.

The next day, Karim came to the house. Mallory let him in before Paula could stop her. "I don't want you here," Paula said.

Karim said, "I just want to see Mallory and Ali. That's all."

Mallory said, "Please, Paula. Let him stay."

If something happened, Paula would be responsible. "All right," Paula said, "but not for long. I'll be right here."

Mallory, Karim, and the baby went out on the deck. Paula watched from the den, her hand on her cell phone in her pocket, just in case. Karim and Mallory talked and played with the baby. They laughed. Mallory cried a little. Karim stayed an hour. When Mallory walked with him to his car, he kissed her, and for a moment Paula thought Mallory would get in the truck with him and leave. She didn't.

Before Barry's accident, Paula had thought she might be the one to go, not Mallory. Now, she felt sure that Mallory would leave. Paula would try to stop her—for Barry's sake or for her own, she didn't know.

Mallory came back in the house and sat at the kitchen table while Ali nursed. Paula had expected drama and tears, but there were none. "You can stay here, you know," Paula said, "as long as you want. You can work on your GED. I can help you."

Mallory didn't answer. Was she even listening? If Paula told Mallory her own story, maybe she could make her understand how important some decisions turn out to be, how they haunt you for the rest of your life.

"Mallory? I want to tell you something."

Ali nestled against Mallory's shoulder. She was patting his back. "What is it?"

Mallory would be a good mother, Paula thought. "Never mind," Paula said. "It can wait."

The baby slept. Paula went about the business of heating up leftovers. A soiled burp pad lay on the table, but Paula hardly noticed the smell. It seemed tolerable now. Consoling.

FROM THIS DISTANCE

Iris stands at the stove stirring plum jelly, watching the thick, white foam rise to the surface. It's almost time to skim. She pushes a strand of damp hair out of her eyes with the back of her hand. The heat's worse today, even after the rain struck the house last night in horizontal sheets and the wind took shingles off the woodshed roof and a big limb off the oak tree next to the barn. Peter is out there now, working at clearing the limb. Iris watches him from the kitchen window. He has taken off his shirt, and even from this distance, she can see the muscles work in his back and arms as he hacks at the limb that's almost as thick as he is, lifting the ax high over his head and bringing it down hard. She thinks about the special supper she's planned for tonight and the red dress hidden away in its box under the bed in the guest room.

The hiss of overflowing jelly startles her. She turns the flame down, skims the surface with a wooden spoon, and drops the scum into an old coffee can. She tests the jelly, watches it coat the silver spoon and drip slowly back into the pan. She ladles it into the sterilized jars lined out on clean white towels on the kitchen table and pours hot paraffin on top.

While the jelly cools, she pours herself a glass of water straight from the faucet and drinks it. She makes two ham sandwiches for Peter's lunch and puts them in his metal lunch box, along with an apple and a slice of homemade chocolate cake. The rhythm of habit feels good.

Iris touches the paraffin lightly with one finger to see if it's cool enough to seal. She screws the lids on tight, picks a jar, and holds it up to the sunlight that makes bright squares on the gray linoleum. The color's good, a clear, deep pink. She holds it higher so that it catches the sun itself, like watching an eclipse through a piece of smoked glass. The sun appears small and dark. Iris sets the jar down quickly, as though it burned her.

She puts ice and water into a Mason jar, picks up the lunch box, and walks out to the tree. Peter has reduced the limb to a stack of firewood and a big bundle of kindling. He stands, stretches, and drags a handkerchief out of his back pocket and mops his face. "Another hot one, Iris," he says as she hands him the jar.

"It sure is. I'm done with the jelly. We can start on the tomatoes by Friday. Or as soon as you think they're ready." Silence hangs in the air between them like dust. When Iris senses his eyes on her, she feels loose inside, like all her bones are pulling apart.

Peter pours a little of the water from the jar onto his handkerchief and wipes his face again. "Are you okay?" he says. "You don't look so good." He pushes her hair back and wipes her face, too.

"I'm all right. The house is so quiet, that's all."

He squints at the sun, then out across the fields. "Well," he says. "I've got to finish up here and get on out to the corn. If I don't hook up the last of the irrigation pipes today, we're going to lose fifty acres, maybe more." He stuffs the damp handkerchief in his pocket. "You go on in and rest a little while. I'll be back before sundown." He puts both hands on her shoulders and kneads them gently. "Go on," he says.

"Sure," Iris says, forcing a smile. "I'll be fine." She sets the lunchbox down and turns and walks back to the house. The screen door slams a little too hard. She leans against it and watches as Peter cranks the tractor and drives off down the gravel road. The house is quiet except for the loud ticking of her grandmother's clock. Iris takes a deep breath and looks around the kitchen as though it's still an unfamiliar place.

They had bought this farm soon after Peter came back from Korea. They'd spent three years working on the rundown house. He'd painted the outside and rebuilt the porches; she'd made curtains and slipcovers and painted most of the inside rooms herself. When they found out she was pregnant, Peter forbade her climbing ladders, and he wouldn't let her go down to the basement. The steps were too steep, he said, for her to be going up and down. Even after he'd repaired the railing, he still insisted she stay off the stairs. "We can't be too careful," he'd said.

Today, she can go down them without having to worry. She loads the jelly jars in a white oak basket. The stairs are dark, but she doesn't turn on the light. Light filters through one dirty little window high on the east wall. She stands on the second step until her eyes adjust to the darkness and then eases down one step at a time, feeling for each one before she moves to it.

Carved out of red clay and left unfinished, the cellar stays cool and damp even in the summer. Moisture collects on the walls like beads of sweat. Iris likes this place that smells like corn fields after days of rain when the corn has begun to mildew in its husks and go to ruin. On wide shelves cut into the earth are her jellies and jams, canned tomatoes, cucumber pickles, homemade corn relish, watermelon pickles—enough to last them for years. She sets her basket down and stacks some of the old jars to make room for these new ones. She takes a jar of plum jelly down and looks at the date: July 1955; their first summer in the house. She walks over to the little window and holds it up to the light. Still good. Not cloudy at all.

They had decided to have the baby at home, but in her last month, Peter changed his mind. What if Dr. Henderson couldn't get there, he said. Maybe they could try a home delivery next time, but not with the first one. So they'd gone to the hospital in the middle of the night when she was still in early labor.

Nobody could explain why the baby boy didn't breathe on his own. Everything had seemed perfectly normal right up to the last minute, but Iris had known something was wrong even before they gave her a general anesthetic. When she woke up, she was in a private room, Peter sitting beside her. From the look on his face, she knew; he didn't have to tell her. He lay beside her in the bed and cried.

They named him Peter John. Peter took care of the arrangements. Both he and Dr. Henderson insisted that she not go to the graveside service, that it would be too hard on her. "No harder than having him and then not having him," she argued, but they prevailed.

When she got home from the hospital, she went first to the baby's room. Peter had already moved the crib and stored it in the barn. "Don't worry," he said, "it'll be safe and dry. I made sure." The room looked oddly empty, even though the rocking chair, the single bed, and the little chest she'd planned to use as a changing table were still there. She felt vaguely nauseated, something she'd hardly ever felt when she was pregnant. She sat down in the rocking chair. "I didn't clean out the drawers," Peter said. He walked over to the window and looked out across the fields. "I didn't know what to do with the stuff—whether you'd want to keep it or not. Some of it is still in the packages, just like it came."

Poor Peter, she thought. "I know," she said. "I'll take care of it."

And she did. As soon as Peter left the house the next morning, she found a couple of old dress boxes and she began packing everything away. She took all the baby clothes she'd so carefully washed ahead of time out of the drawers and laid them on the bed in neat rows. She lingered over a little white sweater her grandmother had knitted; she picked it up and pressed it over her face, inhaling the smell of Ivory Snow. That's what the baby would have smelled like, she thought, that and baby powder and sour milk. There were day gowns she'd made herself, little sacques she'd embroidered, stacks of diapers. She gathered as many things as she could hold in her arms and sat in the rocking chair, rocking gently, pressing them hard against her swollen breasts, wondering why she couldn't cry. Finally, she laid everything in the boxes lined with fresh tissue paper and sealed them. The unopened things—a few blankets, sheets, and pads; little cotton shirts and sleepers in bigger sizes that she'd planned to save until the baby grew into them—she put into an old shopping bag. She'd bought most of it at Gordon's in town. She still had the receipts. It would be practical to take it all back. She wondered if Mr. Gordon would refund the money, or would he refuse, thinking her a bad person if she could make such a deal with her dead baby's things? But there were the hospital bills and the graveside service to pay for. As soon as she could drive, she would take everything to town and ask Mr. Gordon.

The day Iris drove into town, she was fine until she parked in front of Gordon's. When she picked up the bag, something weighed her down; she couldn't get out of the hot truck. She rummaged through the bag, strewing little packages all over the front seat. There was something she should have done, but she didn't. What was it? Then she remembered: she hadn't held him. That was the thing you were supposed to do, no matter what; but they had put her to sleep, and when she woke, the baby was gone.

She had no idea how long she sat there crying before Lucille Parker, an old lady who attended their church, came to the truck. Lucille clucked over her, gave her a handkerchief, and went on and on about how she'd lost a child once, only it wasn't her first. All the time she talked, Iris was fighting to breathe. Iris told Lucille she had a doctor's appointment, gathered up the baby things, and went inside.

Mr. Gordon wasn't as understanding as she'd hoped he might be. He wouldn't give her the money back, but he'd give her credit, he said, that she could use for anything else in the store whenever she was ready. She wanted to tell him how much they could use the money right now, but she didn't think Peter would want her to do that. So she settled for the credit.

On her way out of the store, she saw the red dress in the window display. Going in, she'd been too distracted to notice, but there it was, the prettiest dress Iris had ever seen. For a moment, she longed for it. She shook her head, got in the truck, and drove home.

That night, she sat beside Peter on their bed and stroked his hair. "Peter?" He didn't look up from the *Farm Journal* he was reading.

"What?" he said.

"Peter, I need to talk. Please."

He turned the magazine face down on the bed and took his glasses off, wiping them on his tee shirt. "It's after ten, Iris. I've got to be up at four. Can't it wait?"

"Move over," she said. She crawled in beside him, fitting herself to the length of his body. She was conscious of how soft her belly still felt, but her breasts had gone down considerably. Even though Dr. Henderson had given her a shot to prevent it, her milk had come in on the third day. She had stood over the bathroom sink and cried as she expelled her milk and watched it run down the drain.

She ran her finger down Peter's arm. "Don't," he said.

"Why? What's wrong?" She took her hand away and sat up.

"It's too soon, you know that. We can't make love yet."

"Oh," she said. "Is that what you thought? It is too soon. I need to talk to you, that's all." She took a deep breath. "There's something I need to know."

"What's that?"

"You saw the baby, didn't you?"

Peter put his hand up as if she were about to strike him. "Oh, Iris, please don't."

"I think I'd feel better, knowing that you did." She looked down at her hands in her lap, palms up, empty. "I didn't get to hold him. I should've gotten to hold him, at least."

Peter turned away. "I can't talk about him right now. Not yet."

"I don't even know what he looked like," she whispered. "Can't you tell me that?"

Peter got up, walked to the closet, pulled out a pair of jeans and a shirt, and went into the bathroom.

Iris sat on the side of the bed. "What are you doing?"

"I don't know. I need to get out for a while." He was zipping his jeans, pulling on his boots. He sat beside her. "It's not you, Iris. I just feel so damn bad." He kissed her on the mouth, and then he was gone. She heard the back door slam, the pickup start, and gravel spray as he pulled out down the drive.

Iris lay awake until dawn, listening for the sound of the truck. At first light, she got up and went to the barn to take care of the cows.

Peter came home, but he never told her where he went. They didn't speak of it.

When she went into town for her six-week checkup, Dr. Henderson gave her what she supposed was his standard speech in a situation like hers. "You're young and healthy, Iris," he said. "There's no reason why you and Peter can't have a healthy baby." Without looking at her, he told her it would be fine to make love whenever she felt like it. She could hardly wait to get out of his office.

She hadn't planned to buy the dress, but when she drove past Gordon's, it was still in the window. It couldn't hurt to try it on. When she asked to see it, the saleswoman looked at her oddly; Iris had known her in high school, so the woman knew about the baby. Iris told her that the dress was for her brother's wife, a birthday gift he'd asked her to pick out. She took it into the dressing room and tried it on. When she looked at herself in the mirror, it seemed the woman looking back was someone Iris had known a long time ago and almost didn't recognize.

They had forty-three dollars in credit at the store; Iris spent thirty-five dollars on the dress. She would surprise Peter; she would fix a special supper and dress up, like she used to, and he would like it. "Please let him like it," she said aloud in the car on the way home. "Please."

~ ~ ~

Iris unloads the last of the jelly jars and climbs the basement stairs. Leaving her basket on the kitchen table, she goes to the guest bedroom and takes the dress box out from under the bed, opens the box, and unfolds the tissue. The silk dress isn't fire engine red, but something different: maybe the color of maple leaves in late October. She lifts it out of the tissue and holds it up. It's so sheer that sunlight filters through it. She can't resist trying it on again. She unbuttons her cotton dress and lets it drop to the floor. The red dress floats down over her body like water. She can only see herself from the hips up in the mirror, but the dress looks fine. She feels pretty in it.

All afternoon, Iris prepares supper. She gathers fresh tomatoes, cucumbers, and onions from the garden and makes Peter's favorite buttermilk dressing. She puts a ham in the oven and makes bread, potato salad, and a lemon icebox pie. She sets the table in the dining room with their wedding china and puts a basket of daisies in the middle. She bathes, puts on a little makeup, dresses, and pins her hair up the way Peter likes it. By the time she hears him pull up to the barn on the tractor, she's been ready and waiting for an hour.

When Peter walks in, he slaps his keys on the kitchen counter and drops into a dinette chair, rubbing his hands over his face hard. He looks up. "Where'd you get that dress?" he asks.

Iris smiles, but she feels the stirring of what she'd felt in the yard that morning, that at any moment she might simply fly apart. "At Gordon's," she says, keeping her voice steady. "It's been a while since I was able to wear something pretty like this." She smoothes her hands down the front of the dress. "Feel it," she says, "feel how soft it is."

Peter scrapes the chair back, goes to the refrigerator, and takes out a beer. He rummages through a drawer for the opener, tosses the top into the trashcan under the sink. "I see. How much did you pay for it?"

"I didn't, really." She hadn't thought about having to explain about the credit. "I paid for it out of—"

"How much, Iris?" Peter waggles the beer bottle at her. "Too much?"

Iris drops her eyes, clenches her fists behind her. "I don't see what—"

"Honey, you'll have to take it back. We can't afford anything extra right now, with the hospital bill and the funeral—not until I see for sure what the crops do. It's too risky, you know that." He drains the bottle and drops it in the trashcan. "You *know* that, Iris."

"I know, but I thought it would be nice if we—if I— fixed myself up a little. I thought—"

"Never mind what you thought. Go take it off before you get something on it and they won't take it back. Anyway, what do you need a red dress for? You sure can't wear it to church. It's cut too low."

Iris lowers herself into a chair. This isn't the way things are supposed to go, not at all. She fingers the skirt. So soft. Tears well up, and he sees. He walks over to her and pulls her face to him, resting it against his belly. "I know you want it. Maybe later," he says, "maybe next spring, you can buy yourself something special, but not now." He lifts her chin so she has to look at him. "Now go take it off." He backs away from her. "I'm going to take a shower. Supper smells good," he says, and walks out of the room.

Iris says, loud enough for her voice to follow him, "I thought—" Her voice catches and she clears her throat. "What I thought was, if you went away again, you'd take me with you, and I could wear it then." But Peter must not have heard her. She can hear the water running already.

She sits still for a minute, then stands up heavily and walks to the kitchen, feeling more cumbersome than when she was pregnant. She can't take the dress off, not yet.

Supper, he'll be ready for supper in a few minutes. She opens the refrigerator, pulls out the platters of food, and carries them to the dining room table. She stands back and looks at all of it: ham, tomatoes, potato salad, bread—he'll want something sweet with the homemade bread; how could she have forgotten that?

Iris opens the door to the cellar and stands at the top of the steps. The light from the kitchen illuminates the stairs about halfway down, but the little window below has turned deep blue in the twilight, and the cellar is dark. She shivers. She flicks the light switch just inside the door, and a single bare bulb casts its harsh, unsteady circle of light on the room below.

She goes down carefully. She scans the jars on the shelves; unable to decide what Peter might like, she takes several: muscadine jelly, plum jelly, blackberry preserves, strawberry jam. She climbs the stairs, cradling the jars against her breast with one hand, holding tightly to the rail with the other. As she steps into the bright kitchen, she reaches back for the light switch. One jar slips, then a second, both of them shattering, spattering jelly and preserves and bits of glass all over the kitchen floor, all over her legs, all over the skirt of the red dress.

Coming out of the bathroom, Peter hears the sound of breaking glass.

WIVES

I'm waiting on my front porch out of the rain when my ex-husband Rick and his fourth wife Sherry drive up. Sherry gets out of their SUV with a big umbrella.

"Stay there, Beth. I'm coming to get you!" she shouts through the downpour. I meet her halfway down the walk. Sherry is not going to tell me what to do.

"Be careful, it's slippery," she says. She takes my tote bag and pulls me under her umbrella so mine tangles with hers. When we get to Rick's Tahoe, she opens the back door, throws the bag in, takes my elbow and gives me a boost inside. My flimsy little umbrella sticks, and she stands there in the rain until I get it closed. She slams my door and climbs in the front. I'm pretty dry, but I bet she's drenched.

Rick says, "*Hey*, Beth," like I'm an old buddy he hasn't seen in years.

"Hi yourself, Rick."

He eases down my steep driveway, and once we're out on the flooded streets, he creeps along, the windshield wipers whack-whacking as hard as they can but not doing much good. When he doesn't take the interstate ramp, I can't keep my mouth shut.

"Why don't you take the interstate?" I ask him.

"Old Highway 29 is faster," he says. "No traffic."

Less than an hour ago, I was sitting in my den, waiting out a serious thunderstorm, when my son-in-law Harris called.

"We're in labor," he said. "Laura's doing great. Want to speak to her?"

My heart felt like it might leave my chest. "Sure. Thanks."

At first I thought Laura sounded good. She would, of course—I pictured that determined set of her chin when she's made up her mind to do something—but then I heard the slightest quiver in her voice. I would have crawled to get to her.

A contraction cut the conversation short. "I'll be there as soon as I can," I said, fighting back tears.

I threw some things in a bag. I was sure they'd called her dad, too, even though she didn't say, and I expected the phone to ring any minute and it would be Rick, the master of the friendly divorce, making his gracious offer to pick me up. Well, I didn't need him, and I sure didn't need the new wife.

As I was walking out the door, the phone rang. Thinking it might be Laura again, I picked up without checking the caller ID.

"Hi," Rick said. "Laura call you?"

"Sure. I'm on my way out."

"You shouldn't drive by yourself in this weather, Beth. Especially at night. Let us pick you up."

Us. "No, thanks. I want to take my car in case I need to stay with her."

"She has Harris. You won't need to stay."

"Really, Rick, I—"

"It'll be fine. Sherry doesn't bite." I wondered if she was listening. "We'll be there in ten minutes," he said. "Be ready."

So here I am, feeling like a fool for not standing my ground with Rick, but I have to get to Laura. "Sherry and I were in Memphis a couple of weeks ago," he's telling me now. "Bob and Patty Hester said to tell you hello. We were talking about the time we all went to see Springsteen. The Tunnel of Love Tour, 1988. I'll never forget it."

Sherry says, "You never told me you saw Springsteen." She would have been about ten.

"God, that was something," Rick says. "We could barely buy groceries, but we bought those tickets." He glances at me in the mirror. "We were young and crazy, I guess, weren't we, Beth?"

"I don't know. I didn't go."

"Oh, come on, Beth. Of course you went."

"No, I didn't."

"I would have sworn you were there."

"No. Must have been somebody else," I say. My voice has an edge I don't like.

Rick raises his hand as if to dismiss me. "Okay, okay. Whatever," he says, and I'm remembering how he came home that night with those two tickets, all excited. I thought he'd lost his mind. He was in the last year of his surgery residency. We couldn't afford them, and we didn't have anybody to keep the children overnight. Laura would have been four, Richard just a baby. I told Rick I didn't want to go.

"Fine," he said. "Don't go." So he went without me. I never knew who used my ticket. I never asked.

We ride for a long time in silence, and soon Laura's voice takes the place of Rick's in my head. I want to call her, but I discover I've left my cell phone at home, so I ask Rick to do it.

"Good idea. You have the number, Sherry?"

"Sure." She starts rummaging through her purse.

He says, "You wrote it down, didn't you?"

"Of course I did. I had it with me when we left the house." She turns on the interior light and checks the purse again, the floor, the crevices of the seat, the caddy between them. I have the number, but something's going on here; I wait to see how it plays out.

She shakes her head. "I'm sorry, Rick. I can't find it."

"Beth, do you have it?" He sounds irritated.

"Yeah. Here." I try to hand him the Post-it, but he waves it off and hands his phone to Sherry.

He says to me, "Read Sherry the number," and then to Sherry, "Give me the phone when they answer."

She does, and he drives and talks.

"Put it on speaker," I say, but either he doesn't hear, or he's ignoring me. I lean forward and try to listen. Twice I ask to speak to Laura, but he hangs up.

"Rick, I wanted to talk to her."

"Oh? Sorry." He doesn't offer to call her back, and I'm too stubborn to ask if I can use his phone. "Don't worry, Beth. She's fine, but she's almost eight centimeters. We need to get a move on."

He speeds up, but soon the rain comes in blinding sheets again, and we slow to a crawl. The downpour lasts twenty minutes, and I'm trying to accept that we won't make it before the baby's born when the rain slacks, and Rick turns on his hazard lights and floors it—he must be doing ninety—and cuts the remaining forty-five minutes to thirty. We pull into the hospital parking lot at eleven-thirty.

When we walk into the waiting room, Harris's parents exchange nervous looks. Jack and Louise Parker have been married forever; they probably don't know what to make of the three of us coming in together. We all hug, and

Louise tells us Harris has just come out to give them a progress report.

"Laura's fine," she says. "Just fine."

Like an idiot, I start to cry. I sit down, and Sherry sits beside me and hands me a Kleenex. I really don't know Sherry. She and Rick have been married less than a year, and I've seen them only once, at Laura and Harris's house this past Christmas. She seems so—sincere, is the best word I can think of. Christmas Day, she must have taken a hundred photos. Later, she sent me three framed prints: of Laura (beaming, pregnant), of Laura and Harris together, of our son Richard. In March, she sent flowers on my birthday. It seemed like she was trying to please me, and I couldn't figure out why. Sherry's attractive, of course. Rick always did have an eye for pretty women. His second wife, the woman he left me for, was a knockout, a tall redhead. The third one lasted such a short time she hardly counts. Sherry's petite and blonde like me, but prettier and much younger. I think second wives are much harder to take than subsequent wives. The second one really hurt, but I seem to handle subsequent wives better. Maybe I'm getting used to it.

I take the Kleenex. "This is ridiculous," I say.

Sherry says, "Mothers worry. It's normal." She pats my arm and gets up and joins Rick, who has gone to sit with Harris's father.

Louise comes over, we chat for a minute, and then there's nothing left to say. She goes back to sit beside her husband, and I'm left sitting alone, across from the others. During those first years after Rick left, it would have bothered me, but it doesn't now. I don't have to be alone. There have been men in my life. There was someone a couple of years ago I thought I might be able to love, but it turned out he was a lot like Rick. Or maybe with him, I was a lot like the old me.

We're the only people in the waiting room now. We stare at the walls, glance at each other, look away. I look at my watch. We've been here an hour. I slap a shabby copy of *People* down on the table.

"Why is it taking so long?" I ask nobody in particular.

Rick gets up. "I'll go see what's happening." He heads for the nurses' station. So he still does that, too: glad-hands other doctors whether he knows them or not, charms the nurses. Tonight, I don't mind. Let him.

When Rick comes back, he's carrying a cardboard tray with five coffee cups. "Laura's doing okay. She's just slowed down a bit," he says. "Nothing to worry about. I raided the nurses' coffee. Hope everybody likes it black." Everybody takes some, except Sherry.

"None for me," she says.

He just stands there. "Why not?"

"Rick, you know I never drink coffee late at night."

"Well, you can drink it tonight." He holds the Styrofoam cup out to her. "Come on, Sherry." He sets the cup down on the table beside her.

Sherry picks up the cup and sips the coffee, and I know what I sensed earlier. He used to do the same things to me— shift responsibility, like that business with the phone number in the car, or make me do things I didn't want to do, or try to make me like things I didn't like. Escargot, for example. He would order escargot for me, even though he knew I couldn't stand them. "Once you get used to the idea," he would say, "you'll love them." I never did learn to like escargot.

I watch Sherry turn the cup in her hands. She could be me, all those years ago. I feel tears rising again, and this time, they're not for Laura.

Rick tosses the tray in a trashcan and comes and sits by me. "Laura's in delivery. It shouldn't be long now."

I give him a killer look. "That's easy for you to say. You never had a baby."

"Yeah, but I was there with you both times." To the others he says, "Beth went to the hospital twice in false labor with Laura. And when Richard was born, she must have had the world's longest labor. What was it, Beth? Forty-eight hours?"

He's gotten it wrong. "You've reversed them, Rick. Laura's was the long labor, but you weren't there for most of it. You were on call."

He picks up a magazine and riffles through it. "I was there when she was born, though. Richard, too," he says. "And you *did* have a long labor with one of them."

Harris's mother says, "My babies came really fast, under three hours, start to finish." She smiles too brightly. I want to scream.

Then, at last, Harris comes in, flushed, grinning, teary-eyed. "We have a boy," he says, "eight pounds, six ounces." He shakes his head as though he can't quite believe it.

I feel like I've been underwater, and now I can come up for air. "Laura's all right?"

"She's fine, Beth. Dr. Raynes wanted her to take her time at the last. I'm sorry I couldn't come and tell you, but I didn't want to leave her."

How I want to say, Good for you, Harris. Stay with her. Always. I suppose I could; I doubt Rick would make the connection. But then I look at him, and he's wiping his eyes.

By the time we're allowed in Laura's room, it's nearly two in the morning. I'll never forget the scene: Laura, tired and disheveled but radiant, holding the baby, and Harris sitting on the bed with his arm around her, tracing the crown of the baby's head with his index finger. The picture is so perfect it's painful. My daughter a wife, and now a mother. I think she'll be better at both than I ever was.

Laura looks at me. "Come see," she says.

I walk over, kiss her on the cheek, and move the folds of the blanket to get a look at the baby. He has dark hair that will probably turn light like Laura's did, a turned-up nose like Laura's and mine, Harris's deep dimples, Rick's long fingers. He's perfect, this first grandson of mine. Ours. He's ours.

Harris's mother asks if they've named him.

"Harris Wells Parker," Laura says. She looks up at Harris and smiles. "We may call him Wells, so there's less confusion."

Wells is my maiden name. Rick was probably expecting Richard. If he's disappointed, he doesn't show it.

We all take lots of pictures, and after the Parkers leave, Sherry insists on getting shots of Rick, Laura, the baby, and me, the four of us together.

After the awkward photo session, Laura says, "I was worried about your driving alone, Mama."

"I didn't. I rode with your dad and Sherry."

"Yeah," Rick says, "we came together." He walks over to the window and stands there, looking out, his back to us. Laura looks at me like, What's going on? I shrug.

"Daddy," she says, "don't you think he's beautiful?"

Rick turns around. "Of course I do." He comes back to the bed, bends down, and kisses the top of her head. "And so are you."

Too soon, the nurse bustles in to take the baby to the nursery and tells us we have to leave. Laura and I make plans. When she gets home, I'll come and stay with them for a few days. It feels good to be needed.

I watch from the door as Rick takes Laura's hand and kisses it three times—their signal for "I love you" when she was a child. I get this huge lump in my throat, and I slip out into the hall where Sherry's already waiting.

On our way out, Rick, Sherry, and I stop by the nursery for one last look at the baby. Rick stands behind me and puts his hand on my shoulder.

"They sure made a good baby," he says.

"Yes, they did."

I hear the click and whir of Sherry's expensive camera. Rick squeezes my shoulder. "We made good babies, Beth, didn't we?"

I glance sideways, but I can't see his face. Instead, I see a man and woman who were in the waiting room when we first got there. They make silly faces and coo at one of the other babies. The man has his arm around her, and he's running his thumb along the side of her neck. It strikes me as the simplest, most remarkable gesture of love.

I swallow hard. "That we did, Rick. We made good babies." I turn away from him, and there's Sherry, only she's not taking pictures.

In a few days Sherry will probably send me photographs of Rick, Laura, the baby, and me. I wonder if she'll send one of Rick and me standing at the nursery window, our backs to her camera, the baby barely visible, but I won't need a photograph to remember the weight of Rick's hand, his breath on my neck, his voice close to my ear. I won't need anything to remind me of Sherry's face when I turn around and see her standing there, the camera dangling, her eyes, like mine, full of tears.

"I'm going to find a restroom," I say. "I'll meet you two downstairs in the lobby."

"Wait," she says. "I'll go with you." She says something to Rick that I can't hear and catches up with me.

"Long night," she says.

"You're right about that."

Sherry's face is a mask; the look I saw just moments ago is gone. She just looks tired. I'm tired, too. I had forgotten how exhausting Rick could be.

"And now we have to drive back," I say.

"Yeah," she says. "It'll probably take both of us to keep Rick awake. A job for two women."

In the restroom, we don't talk. I finish first and stand back out of the way while Sherry washes her hands. Her hands look young: no brown spots, no prominent blue veins. I want so much to put my arms around her like I would Laura and tell her that she doesn't have to do it Rick's way, she doesn't have to try so hard. But I don't. I don't think she would believe me. When we walk out into the hall, I look back toward the nursery, but there's no sign of Rick. He's probably downstairs, pacing the lobby. The hall is deserted except for a man who mops a stretch of floor marked off by yellow caution signs and Sherry, who is already halfway to the elevators.

Two more hours in the car. If I know Rick, he'll stop at an all-night station for coffee and a bag of chips. He'll find vintage rock and roll on the radio. He won't let either of us drive.

SIGNS

I took a deep breath and pushed open the door to my mother's room. She was bending over an open drawer of the chest, taking her underwear out, running her hands over slips, bras, and panties, sniffing them or stroking them against her cheek. I watched her put some back and drop others on the floor.

I set the potted lily on the bedside table and tossed the Belk's sack in the closest chair. It was Easter weekend, after all, and I'd felt I had to do something, so I'd brought my mother the white lily—a lovely one with lots of buds—and a dress that snapped all the way down the front so it would be easy for her to wear.

"Hi, Mother," I said. She didn't look up. "Mother?" I said again, a little louder.

She turned. No hello, no glad you're here, Susan, just waving a pair of panties at me. "These aren't mine," she said.

"Let me see." I kissed her cheek, took the panties out of her hands, and checked the sewn-in nametag. They were hers, all right, just dingy from the nursing home laundry. I felt that day's first pang of guilt. I knew there would be more.

"It's that old woman across the hall," she said. "She comes in here when she thinks I'm asleep and swaps her old underwear for mine. I've seen her."

I checked other nametags. All hers. "Mother, Anna Boone lives across the hall. You know her. She was your neighbor."

"No, no," she said, dismissing me with a wave of her hand. "Not Anna. It's the one who dyes her hair that awful red. She ought to be ashamed." With great effort my mother closed the drawer and tugged at the one below it. "Help me clean this one out."

"Did you see the Easter lily?" I said. "Pretty, don't you think?"

She shrugged. "It won't last. Don't know why you'd waste your money on it."

This was not going well. "I brought you a new dress, too. It's navy blue. You love navy." I already had the dress out of the bag and was undoing snaps. "Let's try it on."

She hardly glanced at it. "It's too big," she said.

I turned her to face me and held the dress up to her. "Seems about right." The one she wore had food stains down the front. You'd think they could keep her clean, I thought.

I helped her out of the dirty dress and into the new one. She held the fabric out from her body to show me just how much too big it was. "I told you," she said.

There was so little of her left.

When I was thirteen and believed I would never have breasts, I used to sit on the side of the tub while she bathed. Looking back, it's surprising she allowed me such intimacy. I loved to watch her rise out of the water, her body flushed and glistening. Even though she was past fifty then, her breasts were still high and full, her waist small, her hips a little fleshy, but not what you'd call heavy. That was nearly forty years ago. Now, I hated seeing her drooping breasts, the folds of sagging skin.

"I don't like the color," she said. "It's not navy, it's purple!" She groped at the snaps.

I started to say, No, it's navy, but I stopped myself.

"Where's Maggie?" she asked. "Is Maggie coming?"

There was a time when I would have reminded her my sister was dead, but I'd learned that lying was easier. "Maggie can't come today," I said.

No wonder she wished for Maggie. Maggie was Mother's miracle baby, born when she and my father had been married ten years and had given up hope of ever having a child. I was born nine years later—a miracle, too, after so much time, my mother said—but I'd always believed that had I not been born, Maggie would have been enough.

As Mother had aged, Maggie was the one who picked her up for church, took her out to lunch once a week, did her nails. After Maggie died four years ago of breast cancer, for a while I tried to *be* her. I lived three hours away, but I made that drive every Friday after work and spent weekends with Mother, cooked her favorite foods, took her to get her hair done. But nothing I did was right. "Maggie's pie crust was always so tender, wasn't it, Susan?" she would say, or "Maggie never took this road to the grocery. Are you sure this is right?" I hated Maggie then for leaving me to cope with Mother alone.

She hardly ever mentioned my father. He died when I was four, and it seemed to me that her memory of him was like a great love story she'd read long ago but now only vaguely remembered. Or maybe it was the absurdity of remembering the love of a man who was, in her mind, almost fifty years younger than she. But I had never stopped being hungry for his presence. My memories of him were fragments of light, sounds, smells: the sweet scent of pipe tobacco, laughter, the room whirling when he came through the door at night and swept me up in his arms. We would dance, and then it would be Maggie's turn. He danced with Maggie differently, waltzing her around the room.

After he died, Mother would lie on the couch long past our suppertime. Maggie would make sandwiches for the three of us, pour two glasses of milk, make coffee for Mother, and carry it all on a tray to the dark living room. When Maggie turned on the lamp, Mother would say, "Oh, Maggie! You take such good care of Mother, don't you?"

That's the way it always was, until Maggie died, too.

I helped Mother out of the new dress and into one of hers. She wobbled and almost lost her balance, but I was there to catch her.

"Maybe you ought to lie down," I said.

"I don't want to." Her hands fluttered around her face like she was brushing away cobwebs. "I want to see Maggie."

I steered her towards the bed. "You rest," I said, "and we'll talk."

"All right, but I'm not going to sleep. I sleep too much." She let me help her onto the bed, ease her back against the pillows, lift her legs, and place a baby pillow under her knees. She was light as a child.

She folded her thin arms across her stomach, which always signaled determination. No, she was not going to sleep. "How are you and Hardy doing?" she said. "You should bring him to see me sometime."

She hadn't seen Hardy since we divorced six years ago. "We're fine. He sends his love."

"Is he taking care of you? Your father always took such good care of me."

I held out a strand of my graying hair. "Look at me, Mother. I don't need Hardy. I can take care of myself."

I got up off the bed, walked around it, and stood at the window. There were deep woods behind the nursing home. This time of year, in late March, the trees were turning yellow-green in their tops, and the dogwoods were beginning to bloom, traces of white lace among the dark trees. Signs of spring.

I turned and looked at her. I closed my eyes and tried to superimpose on what I saw, on this almost empty shell of my mother, a different image. In my favorite photograph of her and my father, taken about the time they were married, they're standing beside a car. He's wearing a double-breasted suit and a fedora tilted to one side; she, a broad-shouldered fur coat and high-heeled shoes. Her thick, dark hair is caught up with ivory combs. His arm is around her waist, and they're smiling.

Suddenly, she clutched her stomach and whimpered. "I need to go to the bathroom," she said. "Help me! I can't wait."

We didn't make it in time. I called an aide to help me clean her up and get her into bed. This time, she didn't protest. I read to her until she dozed, and then I put all her underwear away.

I dozed in the chair by the window until a sound like wind startled me awake. A flock of goldfinches—there must have been a hundred of them—covered the patio outside Mother's room. Some pecked at the grass emerging from the cracks. Others clung to the brick walls where the building made an L-shape twenty yards away. I hoped she was still asleep, but she wasn't. She was sitting up, staring out the window.

"Don't be afraid, Mother. They can't hurt us," I said, but then the birds rose up into the air, chattering and circling and swooping. One of them flew into the glass, then another, and another. Like hail stones, these little birds came at the window. I put my arms around her and shielded her eyes until it was over. The whole thing couldn't have lasted more than a few seconds, but my own heart was pounding. I got up to close the blinds and saw the stunned birds floundering on the ground, the rest still diving and calling around them. I snapped the cord hard.

"I've never seen anything like that in my life," I said.

She covered her face with her hands and said, "I have."

I knew what she meant. Over the years, I had heard the story of her father's death so many times. By now I knew it by heart.

The flock of blackbirds had descended out of the eastern sky that cloudless, chilly April morning in 1928. Her father, my grandfather, had gone turkey hunting before dawn. Sometimes, Mother always told me, she put on her brother Byron's old trousers and a wool shirt and went with him, but the night before, her time of the month had come, so she had made excuses. Her father didn't press her, and she blushed to think he might have guessed, or maybe her mother had told him.

Later that morning, her mother walked up to the Jenkins' house half a mile away, leaving Mother to tend the garden. Byron had gone to herd the cows to the back pasture and wouldn't be back until noon. She was hoeing the tender tomato plants when the squawking blackbirds swooped out of the sky and blanketed the garden. Shouting, she ran at them with the hoe, but they taunted and dived at her until she dropped the hoe and ran to the house. She slammed the screen door and latched it and watched the birds strip the young plants bare and forage seeds out of the ground. When there was nothing left, they flew away. She sat down at the kitchen table and still felt their wings flapping around her face. She couldn't stop shivering.

She had seen flocks of migrating birds in winter, when food was scarce and you could feel a change of weather coming. Their foraging then was an omen of snow, and she had seen snow come soon after. But there was no reason in the natural world for what happened that day. An hour later, when she heard the wagon and the shouts just up the road, she knew something terrible was in the air. By the time she got to the front porch, the wagon was pulling into the yard, the horses winded and wild-looking. She recognized three neighbor men who sometimes hunted with her father. They all jumped down, and two of them went around to the back of the wagon. The third one walked towards her. She wondered why none of them would look at her and why her father wasn't with them. And then the two men lifted her father out of the back of the wagon and brought him to the porch. She saw blood, but not until they had laid him on the floor did she see the gaping wound on the right side of his head. They had been hunting up at Mr. Albert's place, one of the men said, his voice coming from far away, and there were others in the woods. Nobody knew where the shot had come from.

Mother always claimed she didn't cry. She knelt on the porch and cradled my grandfather's shattered head in her lap, felt his blood soak through her apron and dress, felt her own blood release and flood the cloth she wore. The three men in overalls stood there, blood-smeared, heads down, their big, rough hands dangling at their sides. One of them asked her where her mother and brother were. He laid his hand on her shoulder and asked a second time before she looked up and realized he was talking to her. She told him her mother was at the Jenkins', her brother in the pastures north of the house. The three men stood out of earshot and talked for a minute, and then two of them left, going in different directions. The third bent down and tried gently to move her away from the body, but she clung tight. She had no idea how long it was before Byron came running around the corner of the house and froze ten feet from her like he too had been shot. In the end, my uncle Byron was the one who persuaded her to let their father go so they could move him inside before my grandmother, her hair undone, her apron flapping, came running and stumbling down the hill, calling my grandfather's name.

That was the story. As far as I knew, it was true. All my life, I had seen my mother's fear of birds first hand. Once when a sparrow got into the house, she locked herself in her bedroom until Maggie managed to shoo it out an open window. I had felt her hands go cold with sweat at the sight of a cardinal. I had seen her shut windows to keep out the song of birds. Later, whenever she came to visit me, I would take down my feeders and store them away until after she'd gone.

I poured a cup of water for her. I steadied it with my hands wrapped around hers, her knuckles twice the normal size, her nails yellow and thick, her skin webbed with wrinkles and veins. She took a sip and pushed the cup away. I set it on the bedside table.

"I remember a time when you were brave," I said.

She cut her eyes at me. "I was always brave."

I took one of her hands in both of mine and stroked it. "I know you were. I mean one particular time, about birds. Do you remember the time our old Persian cat—Delilah, remember her?—brought a baby bird to the back door?"

She nodded. "Cats always bring things to the house. Was she a sweet cat?"

"Yes, she was. But the time I'm thinking about, she wasn't so sweet. I was five, maybe six; I'm sure it happened after Daddy died. I heard Delilah crying at the back door, and I yelled for you but you didn't answer. Delilah kept up this awful moaning, so I went to see what was wrong, and there she was, standing at the bottom of the steps with a baby bird in her mouth. When I opened the door, she looked up at me, so pleased with herself, and she laid it on the ground and crouched beside it. The bird was no bigger than the palm of my hand, and limp, and I remember wondering if that was what dead was like. Then one of its legs fluttered, and Delilah edged closer to it. I yelled at Delilah, and she backed off."

Mother said, "Maggie saved a bird once. I never liked birds."

Maggie. "Mother, I saved the bird. Maggie wasn't home that day. And you know what you did? I kept yelling, and when you finally came, you took one look at that bird and slammed the door! I tried the knob, and when I couldn't open it, I thought you'd locked me out."

"Maggie wasn't there?"

"That's right. That poor bird was all wet and bedraggled, but I didn't see any blood. I knocked and called again, but you didn't answer, so I picked up the bird and sat down on the top step. Delilah crouched a couple of feet away, watching. The bird was so still; I breathed on it in my cupped hands and talked to it. And then I heard the door open, and there you stood, behind the screen, with a shoe box in your hands."

"I found that box for you." She looked at me. "I helped you."

"Yes, you did. You opened the door just enough to give me the box. You had lined it with a scrap of flannel. You still wouldn't let me bring the bird inside, but you boiled some sugar water, and after it cooled, you found a medicine dropper and showed me how to feed it."

"What happened to it?" she said.

There was no escaping it; I had to tell her. "I tried to save it, but it died."

We still sat side by side on the bed, and this time, I was the one who leaned on her. I put my head on her shoulder, and she stroked my hair. She said, "We were all brave, weren't we? You and Maggie and I."

I couldn't speak.

She straightened, and I sat up, too. She pointed at the closed blinds. "I wish the birds would go."

"I know. So do I." I peeked out the blinds and watched the birds feed for a minute longer, and then, as if on signal, ascend as a flock into the bright blue sky.

"I hear them," she said. "They're flying away, aren't they?"

I let the slat drop and turned around. "They're gone."

When I put my arms around her again, I felt her shoulder blades, sharp and wing-like, felt the rise and fall of her breathing, the slight, irregular beating of her heart.

It was time for me to go. Saying goodbye was always difficult. Usually, she seemed to anticipate my leaving long before the time actually came, but that day was different. She hugged and kissed me, but she didn't cling. I stopped in the doorway and looked back at her, standing beside her bed. She raised her hand and waved. I blew her a kiss and let the door swing shut behind me.

What I didn't know then was that a few days later, she would fall in the bathroom and lie on the floor for a while before one of the nurses found her. A week of bed rest would lead to pneumonia, and she would begin to drift away from me. By then it would be April, and everything in the world would seem in the midst of resurrection except my mother, curled on her side in the fetal position, her face resting on the palm of her hand, her mouth an open O, her breathing surprisingly even, the only other sound in the room the tick of the machine that delivered the drip. There would be nothing left for me to do but wait and watch her in this deep sleep. I would open the window a little. There would be a hint of chill in the clean, new air, and in the distant woods, birds calling.

BOOK OF LIES

Downhill

Poised at the top of the ski slope, Robin looked down. Her husband, Howard, waited a few yards below her. This trail was a *blue*. For beginners, he had assured her.

Howard shouted, "Angle across the slope, not down it!"

Robin took a deep breath and pushed off with her poles. She picked up speed.

Howard was skiing alongside. "Okay! Now, make a V with the skis."

She locked her knees, nudged her ski tips together, and made the wedge.

"That's good! You're making a right turn, so lighten up on the right ski and shift your weight to the left."

She tried to do what he said, but her skis drifted apart.

"Weight on the *left* ski!"

"I *know!* " Instead of making the turn, she skidded sideways down the slope and landed in a drift near the trees.

Howard skied to where she sat. "For God's sake, don't cry!"

"I'm not. My nose is running."

One ski had come off. Robin released the other and jabbed her poles into the snow. When she tried to stand, Howard grabbed her arm, but she jerked away and struggled to her feet. "This part I can do. I'm going in."

"You'll catch on."

"I don't think so." She wiped her eyes on her sleeve. "You should go ski with Carl."

At eleven, their son Carl was a natural. He'd been making parallel turns since his first day in ski school. He was skiing with friends while Howard tried to teach Robin what a private instructor hadn't been able to do in three lessons.

Howard took off his gloves and goggles and rubbed his eyes. "You sure?"

"Yeah."

He put the goggles and gloves back on. "Okay, then." He skied away from her, making clean, sharp turns down the slope and a sweeping stop at the bottom. He headed for the lift and didn't look back.

Robin hated the cold and the snow. She hated feeling clumsy and watching Howard eye pretty women in spandex, flying headlong down the slopes or draped on the leather couches around the hotel fireplace. She hefted her skis and poles over her shoulder and trudged through the snow. People skied past her. One guy stopped and asked if she needed help. She forced a smile and said no.

That morning, their younger son, David, had cried and begged not to go to the ski school, but Howard had made him go. Robin could see the lodge below and the little kids on the bunny hill. It wasn't hard to spot David. He would go a few feet and sit down. She couldn't see the look on his face, but she didn't have to. She would take him out of the school and they would do something fun. He was only six. He had plenty of time to learn to ski, if he ever really wanted to.

Back at the hotel, Robin and David drank hot chocolate in front of the lobby fireplace. She tried to call her sister, Laurel, but got no answer. The room phone was ringing as she unlocked the door. When her brother-in-law, Paul, said her name, she knew. Something had happened to Laurel.

The Drive Home

They checked out of the hotel as soon as they could pack. The trip home to Memphis took eighteen hours. Around four in the morning, Howard was all over the road, driving across the reflectors that divided the lanes, weaving into the breakdown lane. It made Robin crazy. She insisted she drive. It was better than thinking. The rush of passing eighteen-wheelers slammed their Honda like hard gusts of wind. She kept a white-knuckled grip on the steering wheel and tried not to picture her sister dead.

Molly

Robin left Howard and the boys to unpack the car and went straight to Laurel's house.

"I'll come over as soon as I get cleaned up," Howard said.

"Please don't. Stay with the boys. What can you do?" She walked away before he could answer.

Laurel and Paul's tiny bungalow sat on a tree-lined street in a quiet old neighborhood. One of Laurel's friends met Robin at the door. Paul sat in the den, ashen and shaky. He stood and hugged Robin and held on for a long time.

When he let her go, she said, "Where's Molly?"

He looked around. "Playing. Somewhere."

Robin found Molly under the dining room table, curled up with her favorite blanket, sucking her thumb. Robin crawled under the table. "Hey, Molly."

Molly looked up at Robin. "I can't find my mommy."

Robin pulled her onto her lap. "I know, baby. I know."

She held Molly and breathed in the baby shampoo scent of her hair. Robin wanted Laurel to walk in that room, to look under the table, and say, "*There* you are! I've been looking for you!" Laurel's absence knocked the breath out of her. She held on to her sister's child and cried, silently, so Molly wouldn't hear.

Stories

What Paul told Robin: he had called Laurel from the hospital around noon, and she'd sounded so good. Not depressed at all. He called a couple of hours later, and when nobody answered, he thought Laurel had taken the children out for a walk. When he kept trying and still got no answer, he asked another intern to cover for him and went home. He found Laurel in the tub, naked, submerged, and three-month-old Jack, his head nestled face down between her breasts. There was an empty bottle of antidepressants on the floor. He should have counted the pills, he said. He should have locked them up. The coroner had come and gone. Laurel's death would be ruled a suicide, Paul said. "But the baby's death is considered a homicide. Can you believe that?"

What Robin told herself: she shouldn't have gone on

the ski trip with Howard. It hadn't fixed the marriage. It hadn't fixed anything.

After

Paul asked Robin to take care of Molly until he could find a nanny willing to stay nights. Molly could go back to day care, but he was on call every third night and every other weekend. Robin had known it was what she wanted before Paul asked. She couldn't bring Laurel back, but she could take care of the child.

Paul would finish his internship the end of May. He had applied for an internal medicine residency at several hospitals, all out of state. He would take Molly with him, or he might send her to live with his parents, a thousand miles away. Either way, she would lose Molly. For now, though, Robin could have her.

She called her school's principal to ask for an extended leave of absence. He told her not to worry, to take all the time she needed. She didn't discuss it with Howard. When he came home from his law office the next afternoon, Robin was sitting in the den reading to Molly. He didn't seem surprised.

"Hi, Punkin'," he said to Molly, went to the kitchen, poured himself a bourbon.

Paul tried three live-in nannies. Each time, after a week or two he brought Molly back to Robin. By then it was May, and he had accepted a residency in St. Louis, three hundred miles away. He asked Robin to keep Molly a while longer. "I'll take her as soon as I get settled and can find decent help."

When Robin hesitated, her voice choked with tears,

the *yes* stopped in her throat, he said, "If you can't do it, I'll work something out." He got up and looked out Robin's kitchen window. Carl was pushing Molly on the swings in the back yard. "I want her. You know I do. It's just . . ." He turned and raised his hands, helpless. "God, she's so much like Laurel, you know?"

So Paul moved, and Molly stayed. It was Laurel she missed. "I saw Mommy," she'd say.

The first time, Robin was stunned. "You did? Where?"

Molly saw her mother everywhere: in the backyard sandbox, on the swings at the park, in Molly's room at night, telling her stories that Molly repeated to Robin. Molly never mentioned her baby brother. Then one day, she simply stopped talking about Laurel. Robin gathered all the photos she could find of Laurel and Molly together, and Paul, too, from before Molly was born to the most recent ones that included Jack. They were happy pictures, Robin thought. She put them in an album and used it like a picture book to tell Molly stories, sometimes real, sometimes invented. She hoped the stories would help Molly remember Laurel, but if she were honest, she knew the stories were really for her, for keeping Laurel alive.

The First Summer

Sunlight on water. Relentless wind, flotillas of thunderheads, rain in the afternoons. Molly digging in the sand where the waves make foam, Robin beside her. Carl and David flying kites, swimming, catching crabs. Just Robin, the boys, and Molly, empty spaces where Laurel should be, and Howard too, living in an apartment since the first of July. Finding himself, he said.

Stepmother

The summer Molly turned six, Paul brought his fiancée, Claire, for a visit. Claire was everything Laurel had not been: tall, model-thin, outgoing. She dressed well. She sold real estate. There were trips to the zoo, the parks, movies. Robin told herself she had to give Claire a fair chance. She waited all week for Paul to tell her when he and Claire planned to take Molly. Finally, the day before they were leaving, she asked him.

"Not right away," he said. "We'll need some time." After the wedding in August, a month went by, and another.

Robin had resigned from her teaching job a couple of months after Laurel died. She hadn't been able to bring herself to put Molly in daycare. The divorce had been civil, and Howard was generous. Robin could afford to stay home, but she felt guilty; her own sons had gone to daycare while she taught and stole a few hours here and there to paint in a little rented studio. She justified her choice to stay home with Molly. Her boys had *had* her; Molly's mother was gone.

After Molly started kindergarten, Robin taught a couple of art classes three mornings a week at a community college. She bought new oils and canvasses, and on the other mornings, those long hours without Molly, she painted for the first time in two years. The paintings she finished, she hid away. One of them started out as a portrait of Molly but had turned out to be Laurel at five instead, unsmiling, wistful, looking off at something beyond the canvas.

When Molly entered first grade, Robin took a job teaching art at the Catholic high school. She liked having a routine. A routine would be good for Robin when Molly went to live with Paul and Claire.

Molly didn't leave, though. Paul and Claire had decided a move over Christmas would be easier. Then Christmas became just another visit, and when Paul brought Molly home, she was subdued. She had reverted to sucking her thumb.

Robin confronted Paul. "It's not fair to Molly. When is she moving?" It's not fair to me, she thought. Paul was selfish, selfish.

He looked miserable. "Molly's not happy there. I keep hoping—"

"You hope what? You take her and you love her. She'll adjust."

"Look, it's complicated. Claire's . . ." He smoothed his hands on his trousers. When he didn't look at Robin, she understood.

"You mean Claire doesn't want her."

He shook his head. "Claire says having Molly will be like having Laurel in the house. She says I'm still attached to Laurel."

Robin felt a guilty rush of satisfaction. She hadn't liked Claire from the beginning.

Paul said, "She's given me an ultimatum. It's her or Molly."

"And you choose Claire? How can you do that?"

"I told you, it's complicated. I love Claire. I know it sounds trite, but it's a chance at a new life." He picked up a photo of Laurel off the table and one of Molly next to it. "I'm not sure I can do it. Ever."

He left without saying goodbye to Molly. He said it was better that way.

Molly at Seven

Molly was under her bed. Robin tried to coax her out while Paul waited downstairs to take her to St. Louis for her summer visit. Six long weeks. "I don't *want* to go!" Molly said.

"Sweetie—"

"I don't like Claire!"

"Molly, don't be that way. Your daddy will be so disappointed if you don't go."

"I will, Molly," Paul said.

Robin hadn't heard him come in. She mouthed, "You try."

"Come on out, Molly." Paul got down on the floor. "Well, I guess I have to stay right here until you come out, baby girl."

Molly kicked the bedsprings above her. "I'm *not* a baby."

"Oh? Big girls don't crawl under the bed and hide from their daddies."

Robin stood back and watched. Paul was halfway under the bed now, talking to Molly. Robin couldn't hear what he was saying. Finally, he crawled out, then Molly.

"That's my girl," he said. He gathered her into his arms and brushed tears off her cheeks. "Hey, it's going to be fine. You can talk to Aunt Robin and the boys every day." He looked up at Robin. "Right, Aunt Robin?"

"Right," she said, but it irritated her. She had never been Aunt Robin; with Molly she was just Robin.

Molly's things were already in the car. Paul carried her down the stairs. The departure happened as Robin had imagined it: she and Carl and David on the porch waving and smiling, Molly's forlorn little face pressed against the car window. It's only six weeks, Robin reminded herself. And yet she closed her eyes and imagined Molly moving away from her like a lesson in perspective, lines converging until she became a finite point on the horizon and then disappeared entirely.

Molly Now

Molly takes a half-gallon of ice cream from the freezer and eats out of the carton.

"You're late," Robin says. "Where were you?"

"I was at Beth's. I told you. Test tomorrow."

Robin sighs. "Okay. Get to bed."

Molly puts the ice cream away and tosses her spoon in the sink. She walks around the island. It seems she'll do anything these days to keep from touching Robin. She runs up the stairs and slams the door to her room. Robin supposes she should have expected a rebellious streak. It's harder now that it's the two of them, with Carl in grad school and David away at college. Paul's moving back hasn't helped. He and Claire and their two young daughters live in a fine house only a couple of miles from Robin's. They have let Molly decorate her own room in that house, but Paul hasn't asked Molly to move in with them permanently. Robin expects it any time.

"Anything I want," Molly tells Robin. "Paul says I'm getting a car when I turn sixteen."

Robin isn't surprised when Paul calls and says he needs to talk to her. They arrange to meet for lunch at a nice restaurant on Saturday. "My treat," he says.

At the restaurant Paul orders each of them a glass of wine. They make small talk, and Robin wonders when he'll get around to what he really wants. Then he tells her. "Molly wants to move in with us." He shakes his head. "It won't work. She's better off staying with you."

"For God's sake, Paul. What's all this about then—the room, the clothes, the money? No wonder she thinks she can move in. You've been courting her."

"It's not *about* anything. I want her to know I love her. I'll take care of her." He drains his wine glass.

Robin sets her own glass down. "You know she'll blame me if you don't let her." She thinks, Claire. Claire's to blame.

He leans back in his chair. "I'll tell Molly. I'll explain everything."

The following Thursday, the attendance secretary at Molly's school calls Robin and tells her Molly was in her morning classes, but she didn't show up for her sixth period. "She'll have to be disciplined for this, Mrs. Stevens," the secretary says and hangs up.

The knot of anxiety builds in Robin's chest. She waits until after four to call Molly's friends. Nobody's seen her since lunch.

Robin calls Paul's office and leaves a message. He calls back a little after six, and Robin tells him Molly's still not home.

He says, "Don't you think she's probably at a friend's house?"

"Don't you think I've called everybody I know? Come on, Paul."

"Let's not overreact. Did you call Claire?"

She has not. He says he will. He calls Robin back. "She's not there, either. I'm leaving here to make rounds. I'll keep my cell on. Let me know when she gets home."

Robin slams the phone down. She goes around the house and turns on every light. She imagines the house a beacon in the dark, calling Molly home. The door to Molly's room is closed. Robin opens it and finds the light switch. The room is in shambles. Something smells. Incense? Pot? She opens drawers, takes things out, puts them back. She's about to leave when she notices the photograph album she had made for Molly all those years ago, when she first came to live with her. The album is open on Molly's bed, the pages empty, photos in the trashcan beside the bed, all torn into tiny pieces. So much for the stories of a little girl and her happy life.

Lies. All lies.

She dumps the torn photos on the bed. Fragments of Laurel here, Paul there, Molly, baby Jack. She drops them back in the trash, gets up, turns off Molly's light, closes the door, and goes downstairs. She grips the banister. She feels lightheaded, her knees like jelly.

Molly's Absence

Robin waits in the den, turns on the TV, turns it off. Gets up, goes to the kitchen, makes tea, doesn't drink it. Around ten, she hears a car. She looks out. It's Paul and Molly. He puts his arm around her, but she pushes him away. When Robin opens the door, Molly brushes past her, slings her book bag down in the hall, and heads up the stairs.

"Wait just a minute, young lady," Paul says. "You come back here!"

Molly doesn't slow down. A door slams upstairs, and Robin and Paul stand there looking at each other.

"Come in," Robin says. "It's freezing."

Paul drops onto the couch without taking off his coat. He has snowflakes on his shoulders, in his hair.

"Where was she?"

"She wouldn't tell me. She said she failed a geometry test, and that's why she left school. She was at our house by the time I got there. She'd walked. All that way in the cold." He runs his hands over his face. "She was so agitated I thought she might be on something. She said you'd be furious and she couldn't come back here, so could she stay over. I told her no. I said you were worried sick, and she can't treat you this way after all you've done for her."

"Oh, Paul. Why am I always the bad guy?" Something, not sound or movement—a shadow, maybe—makes her turn. Molly stands in the doorway.

"You went in my room," she says. "Don't you ever, ever do that again!" Molly starts back up the stairs, stops halfway, turns. "Why are you still here, Daddy?" Then she's gone.

Robin has never heard her call Paul that.

After he leaves, Robin curls up on the couch. She has no intention of falling asleep. What if Molly slips out? But Molly wakes her at six-thirty. She's dressed for school.

"Will you write me a note?" she says. "Say I got my period and messed up my skirt. I was embarrassed. That's why I left."

Robin writes the note. "Want some breakfast?"

Molly shakes her head. She pulls a paper out of her backpack. "You need to sign this."

It's the geometry test. An F. So she wasn't lying about that. Robin signs it and doesn't comment. "Promise me you'll come straight home."

"Sure." Molly stuffs the test paper in the backpack, grabs her jacket, and she's out the door. Robin watches her run for the bus that's rounding the corner. Robin calls her own school to tell them she'll be late.

Robin grounds Molly. There's some hysteria Friday night over the grounding, and Molly locks herself in her room. Robin leaves trays outside her door that remain untouched.

Truth

Sunday night, Molly comes downstairs. She's drying her hair with a towel. Robin says, "Let me do it." She's surprised when Molly sits down and hands her the towel and a comb. Robin works the comb from the ends to the scalp to get the tangles out, like she used to when Molly was little.

"There," Robin says when she's done.

Molly gets up and goes to the window.

Robin looks out too at the February darkness. "I think I'll make hot chocolate. Want some?" Molly nods.

Robin makes hot chocolate the old-fashioned way—cocoa, sugar, whole milk. She brings two mugs on a tray. "Sit," she says, and Molly does. Robin grips her mug to keep her hands still. It's time. "There's something I need to tell you, Molly."

Molly starts to get up. "I don't need another lecture."

Robin puts her hand on Molly's arm. "Please. Stay."

She tells her then that Laurel's death wasn't an accident, that she killed herself and the baby. While Robin talks, Molly stares at her hands. "She was sick, Molly. None of us knew just how sick," Robin says. "You look like her, but you're nothing like her. Not that way."

When Molly looks up, her gaze is cool, unemotional. "How do you know I'm not?"

"I knew your mother. I know you."

"You think you do." Molly shakes her head. "You thought I didn't know what she did?"

When Robin finds her voice, she says, "Nobody knew. We told everybody it was an accident. Everybody."

Molly bites at a hangnail. "Daddy told me."

Robin can't breathe. "He what?"

"He told me. I was visiting in St. Louis, the summer I was thirteen. I threw a tantrum and broke one of Claire's precious vases. He got angry. He said I was going to be like my mother. He told me what she'd done and how she did it. And then he cried and said he was sorry. He was pathetic. I asked him what he was sorry for—for telling me? And he said no, he was sorry about *her* and about *me*. He made me promise not to tell you I knew."

Molly gets up and crosses to the fireplace and stands with her back to Robin. Robin doesn't know if she can believe her. She wants to call Paul, but he would probably lie.

"We tried to protect you," Robin says.

Molly turns and faces her. "And you try to be my mother, but you're not." She takes a sip of her hot chocolate, sets it down. "Paul and I talked last night. Claire's taken the girls and gone back to St. Louis. He says I can stay with him. For a while, at least."

There's a rushing in Robin's head like wind. *Claire, gone.*

"I'm going. You can't stop me."

"I know that. I wouldn't try. Just please tell me one thing. The pictures in your room— tell me why you tore them up."

Molly looks beyond Robin at the dark window. "I wanted to be rid of her."

Robin's mind reels. "Why now, if you've known for two years?"

Molly shrugs. "At first, after Daddy told me, I'd take the pictures out and go through them. I tried to imagine what my mother would be like if she'd lived, but I couldn't. I kept imagining what she did and how she took the baby with her." Molly's chin trembles. "Why didn't she take me, too? Why, Robin?"

"I don't—"

Molly crosses the room and stops in the doorway. "And you know what else? I don't know if Daddy told me the truth. What I don't understand is why *you* never did."

Call

Molly's been at Paul's a month when she calls Robin at two on a Saturday morning. "Come get me," she says. "Daddy's gone ballistic just because I came in late."

"I can't do that," Robin says.

"What do you mean, you can't?" Molly says.

Robin takes a deep breath. "You need to work things out with your dad."

Robin hears Paul yell, "Give me that phone!" Then, "Hello? Who's this?"

"It's me, Paul. Molly called me."

He sighs. "You don't need to be mixed up in this. I'll call you tomorrow." But he doesn't.

The Last Summer

David comes home for the summer and gets a job working in a restaurant kitchen, but he's in and out of the house with his friends. He watches a movie with Robin occasionally, and he gives her a peck on the cheek when he leaves the house. Robin is happy for the extra cooking, the ringing phone, the music drifting down the stairs.

David asks her how Molly's doing at Paul's.

"I don't know," Robin says. "I don't see her." She's peeling potatoes. She looks up. "It's okay. That's where she needs to be."

"Huh," he says.

In a couple of days, David tells Robin that Molly wants to have lunch. "How's Thursday?" he says.

"With me? I doubt she wants to see me."

He hugs her. "I'll be there, Mom. It'll be okay."

~ ~ ~

Robin's been waiting at the restaurant ten minutes when her cell phone rings.

"Hey," David says. "Molly there yet? I tried her cell, and there's no answer."

"No, she's not. Where are you?"

"I have to work the lunch shift. I can't come."

"Oh, David. You knew you couldn't be here, didn't you?"

"No, Mom. Honest. Tell Molly I'll call her. Gotta go."

Robin looks up and there's Molly, standing in the entrance. Robin waves at her and Molly turns like she might bolt, but then she pulls out her cell phone, walks over, sits down, and fiddles with it for a full minute before she snaps it shut.

Robin says, "Hi, Molly. David's—"

"Not coming. I know. I just got his text." Molly cocks her head. "What do you think? Is this a setup to get us together?" She waggles her fingers in the air like a sorceress.

"I don't know. Anyway, here we are. How are you?"

Molly rolls her eyes. "Claire's back. Did you know that?"

"No, I didn't."

"But it's okay. In fact, I sort of like her. She's stylish, you know?"

So this is what lunch is going to be, Robin thinks, one sting after another. They order. They eat. Robin asks about school and gets yes and no answers.

Then Molly says, "I have to tell you something." The emphasis on *you*.

"Oh? What's that?"

"I'm going away to school in the fall. I thought I should be the one to tell you. No more secrets, right?" Molly looks expectant.

"If it's what you want, Molly, I'm glad." But Robin's not sure it's what Molly wants. It has Paul written all over it, or maybe Claire.

"I'm seeing a counselor. It's one of Dad's *conditions* for living with them. The guy's actually pretty nice. I'm working through some stuff."

Robin feels dull, stupid. Why can't she come up with something to say?

Molly says, "I'm not in trouble. My grades are good. I just want to . . . go somewhere, you know? Away from here." Molly looks at Robin, and for a moment her expression changes, and Robin sees the little girl hiding under the table, wondering where her dead mother was.

When they part, Molly hugs Robin tentatively. Robin sits in her car for a while before she can drive home. When David comes in late that night, she's lying on the den couch in the dark.

"What's wrong, Mom?" he says.

"Don't turn on the light," Robin says. "Sit." He does, and as hard as it is, she tells him the whole story. When she's done, she feels emptied, and oh so much lighter.

The middle of August, David goes back to college. Molly goes, too, to a boarding school in Virginia. Molly calls Robin to say goodbye. At least there's that.

Robin wanders through the house. She goes in each child's room (no longer children, any of them), dusts Carl's sports trophies, straightens David's books. It's Molly's room that's lifeless. Robin is ashamed that she misses Molly most.

At night the empty rooms yawn dark and open like mouths. Robin closes all the doors. She turns on the TV for the noise. She sleeps little and forgets to shower. She stands in her studio and stares at an empty canvas.

She calls Carl. "I need to see you. Is next weekend okay?" He says yes too quickly, and she wonders if David called him. No, she thinks. She's the game player, not her sons.

Molly and Laurel

October. A letter from Molly postmarked Chatham, Virginia. Blank paper. A photograph of Laurel at the beach, holding two-year-old Molly. Sand like snow, water the color of topaz. Laurel's smile, the visible swell of her belly. Robin's sharp intake of breath, the rush of tears. On the back, in Laurel's handwriting: July 1997. Underneath that, in Molly's hand, "You should have this."

A Note from the Author

Sincere thanks to everyone who helped make *Crosscurrents and Other Stories* a reality.

So many fellow participants and leaders in workshops—at The Lighthouse in Denver, Eckerd College's Writers in Paradise Conference, and the Miami-Dade Writers' Institute—have shared their insights and inspired me. One in particular, Antonya Nelson's Advanced Short Story workshop at The Lighthouse in the summer of 2014, changed the way I envisioned and revised several of these stories.

I owe special thanks to Clifford Garstang, editor of *Prime Number Magazine,* and to the other editors who gave some of the stories their first homes. And of course my gratitude goes to Kevin Morgan Watson, Editor and Publisher at Press 53, for considering them worthy as a collection.

Gale Massey, long-distance friend, incisive reader, and marvelous writer, has offered sound advice, held me accountable, and, at times, kept me from burning everything! Here at home, Marion Barnwell's in-depth reads have been invaluable.

Residencies at the Hambidge Center and the Ragdale Foundation afforded much-needed solitude and time for uninterrupted work.

The Mississippi Arts Commission Literary Arts Fellowship I received in 2015 opened doors to opportunities I might never have pursued otherwise.

I can't leave out my "bookgroup"—as savvy a group of women as you could ever hope to meet. They believed.

My extended family has encouraged this dream and dreamed along with me. And finally, my deepest gratitude goes to my husband, Austin Wilson, my best (and toughest) reader, my champion, my love. Without him these stories would not exist.

A seventh generation Mississippian, GERRY WILSON grew up in Pontotoc, a little town nestled in the hill country, in a household with her maternal grandmother, a born storyteller. Gerry's love of story began there. For more than twenty years, she taught English and creative writing to high school students. As she learned how to impart her love of reading and writing to her students, her yen to write fiction blossomed.

Now retired, Gerry writes short and long fiction. Her short stories have appeared in numerous journals. "Mating," the first story in *Crosscurrents,* won the Prime Number Magazine Award for Short Fiction in 2014. In 2015 she received a Mississippi Arts Commission Literary Arts Fellowship. She has studied fiction writing with Antonya Nelson, Ann Hood, Jane Hamilton, Connie May Fowler, Dorothy Allison, and Ron Hansen. She is currently working on a new novel.

Gerry is a wife, mother of four grown sons, grand-mother of seven—four boys and three girls—and step-grandmom to three more boys. Gerry and her husband, Austin, live in Jackson, Mississippi, with their Siamese cat, Oliver.

Cover artist CLAY JONES is a record producer, engineer, and composer from Oxford, Mississippi. He makes solo recordings under the name *Prehistoric Bird* and takes photographs with his iPhone.

CPSIA information can be obtained at www.ICGtesting.com
Printed in the USA
BVOW08s2132090216

436147BV00001B/15/P